THE
WOLVES
ARE
WATCHING

NATALIE LUND

VIKING

VIKING
An imprint of Penguin Random House LLC, New York

First published in the United States of America by Viking, an imprint of Penguin Random House LLC, 2022

Visit us online at penguinrandomhouse.com.

Library of Congress Cataloging-in-Publication Data is available.

Manufactured in Canada

ISBN 9780593351093

10 9 8 7 6 5 4 3 2 1

FRI

Edited by Liza Kaplan
Design by Lily Kim Qian
Text set in ITC Berkeley Oldstyle Pro

For Johnny, with love always

1

LUCE

Waning Cresent (16% visible), Tuesday, October 13

THERE ARE EYES in the woods.

Two points of gold beyond the blue reflection from the TV on our windowpanes and our dandelion-seeded lawn, glimmering among the shadowed trunks. The hairs rise on my arms, prickling with goose bumps. I drop the pencil I'm chewing, the marks of my teeth an ant march down the yellow paint, and punch down the couch pillows so I have a better view of our backyard.

"Mom, what's that?" I ask. She's at the kitchen sink, her hands submerged in soapy water. She had a late client at the salon while I swept up, and she hasn't changed out of her work clothes yet: black clogs that look like nurses' shoes, black pants, and a black button-down, with sleeves rolled to the elbows.

She glances out the window behind the sink. "What?"

1

"Those eyes." I point.

"Probably tricks of light," she says, but she stares hard at the woods, mouth open, her tongue resting on her bottom lip like when she concentrates on cutting someone's hair. In the window reflection, I notice I'm doing the same. I close my mouth.

"What lights could possibly cause that?" I ask her.

She pulls open the dishwasher and plunks some silverware into the basket. "The porch lights, I suppose."

"The porch lights aren't on," I say.

"The TV, the moon, I don't know, Luce."

Her tone says she's tired and to drop it, but the eyes are still there, almond-shaped and shining. My skin crawls with the sensation of being watched. No way they're tricks of light. They are too yellow to be human and too close to the ground to be an owl's. They belong to something large.

I grew up hearing all sorts of stories about the forest behind my house—hikers and their dogs disappearing without a trace, an escaped murderer from the local asylum scratching at campers' tents, pretending to be a branch until the campers fell asleep. And fairies called Vila posing as forest animals, capturing men with their singing, and turning them into trees. But over the years, my best friend and next-door neighbor, Anders, and I have spent hours beneath its canopy within calling distance of our mothers in the summers and early falls. We used to imagine ourselves as talking foxes or warrior centaurs or sibling monarchs of a wooded kingdom. We built castles from fir boughs, complete with leaf moats and branch drawbridges. With the sun filtering through the leaves, we weren't afraid.

Now, though . . .

Are you rehearsing? I text Anders. The fall play started a few weeks ago, and he was, unsurprisingly, cast as the lead— even though we're only sophomores.

The three dots in a bubble appear, and I wait for his response. **Affirmative,** he writes, ever the nerd.

Look out your back window.
On it. What am I looking for?

You'll know when you know, I write.
Cryptic. I like it. A minute passes. **I don't see anything,** Anders texts.

Are you upstairs in your room?
Sure am. Why do you want to know?☻

My cheeks warm. Our texts have been veering in this new direction lately, and I don't know what to make of it, but my body has been responding with flushes and flutters. I take a breath and ignore it.

Look straight behind our house. Do you see
yellow eyes?

Eyes?!?

Yes, eyes.

No. But I can say I do if you want. You might need
someone on your side when they come to take
you to St. Anthony's.

St. Anthony's is Picnic's only point of interest, a long-retired asylum that is now used for overpriced ghost tours. There's a ghost in every empty patient room, according to the legends.

Anders and I have walked the yellowing hallways countless times, and he will begrudgingly admit that, once, we heard the Wailer—the ghost that cries for her missing child. Just remembering that keening sound, high-pitched and echoing down the corridors, makes my stomach feel like I'm on a roller coaster about to drop.

Thanks so much, I text. Super helpful.

As always, my pleasure.

I put down the phone and sit up straighter on the couch. Maybe his room is at the wrong angle to see them. Or maybe a tree is blocking his view.

"What about you?" I ask Giblet, our white French bulldog, who is asleep, curled in her bed by the fridge. "Do you see them?" She loves to chase all manner of wildlife creatures, but she glances at me and sighs like she can't believe I woke her for something so ridiculous.

Mom comes to sit beside me, carrying the scent of hair spray and lemon dish soap, and switches the channel to the local news. She taps my notebook page and the math problems I abandoned when I spotted the eyes. "Finish. It's almost time for bed."

I roll my eyes. What other fifteen-year-old has a bedtime? But I dig my pencil out from where it's wedged between the couch cushions. I finish a few problems for show, and when I look up, I find the eyes again, glowing like distant fires, flickering as the trees bend in the breeze across my line of sight.

What would watch our house at night like this?

A predator. That much I know.

2

FANYA

I WATCH THE dark-furred People Only in their side-by-side Dens. The Boy talks to a tall glass in the upper part of the Den. He repeats the same words over and over. He tosses his mane. He makes different mouth shapes. He lowers the fur stripes over his eyes. He moves his hands, pushing them out from his Form and opening and closing fingers. Is he practicing how to be People like I do? Changing Forms and wobbling on naked fish feet along the stream, trying to make sounds with the thick worm tongue People have?

The Girl leaves the older People Only on the long gray poof and ties a rope to the fat rat dog. A light flicks on when she steps outside. It makes her eyes shine like raindrops caught on leaves. I sniff the wind. She smells like river pebbles.

The Boy stops saying words to the tall glass and watches her too. The dog pees on the grass patch, and the Girl—she looks right at me!

Old One Teodora says we should never be seen. People Only are danger. We could be trapped and kept until we are Gone Forever and mounted on walls. My heart *thump-thump-thumps*, but my tail swishes. I can't help it.

"Hello?" the Girl calls.

Her voice makes my fur stand. I crouch and take off. Run, stopping only at the stream. The Girl and fat rat dog aren't behind me.

I pant and lap water. The moon is a slim talon of white. It is almost time for the Big Hunt—*my* Big Hunt—because the moon will be opening its eye wide for Forefathers' Eve. A rare moment when there is enough magic to add a member to our Pack.

I reach Great Tree and belly crawl underneath her. The Old Ones dug the Den so that her roots hang above our heads for Air Forms to perch on and Earth Forms to wind around. The Den walls still show the Old Ones' claw and talon marks. The floor is lined with skin shed, fur, and feathers. It smells of mushrooms and dead squirrel. I love to roll onto my back and rub my shoulders in it.

The Pack is all here, the Den filled with the *huh huh huh* of panting tongues and the *fwup fwup fwup* of wings and the *sssss* of long bodies against dirt. Danica and Alina swish their tails to see me.

Old One Nina growls, ears back. Her Gray Form is bigger than mine, and her bone-colored fur rises along her spine. She wants to know where I've been.

I groan with a swish of my tail, meaning *hunting*. I *had* been hunting before I saw the side-by-side People Only Dens, bright white and clean like a snowstorm. I couldn't look away.

Ar-er-er, she moans back, a question.

I tuck my tail and drop to the ground, rolling, belly up. I have nothing. Not even a squirrel. I watched the People Only instead of catching food. I don't want the Old Ones to take away my hunt. I want them to see I am strong and fast even though I am youngest.

Old One Teodora slithers over, her Earth Form a light-gold length with dark-brown bands. She heart-decides People, which means she will talk, and changes into one that is milk-skinned, moon-eyed, and white-furred.

"Tomorrow, every moment counts," she says.

I roll back over, chin on my forelegs, and swish my tail, meaning *I can do better. I will.*

Old One Zora perches on Great Tree's root in Air Form, looks down her sharp beak, and lets out a *scree-eee*.

"I agree. You need to learn the Old Ways, Fanya," Teodora says. "Can you do what we have told you?"

I stand and woof.

The hunt is still mine.

IN THE OLD WORLD

IN THE OLD world, we howled, our teeth to the barefaced moon, the leaves shuffling our percussion. The song protected our home, and so we sang, circled together every night. Men wandered, lost and weary, or stalked, lustful and lewd, into our forest. Our song gripped them, the howl wrapping itself around them like a vine. They grew roots where they stood, became barked, thick, and green. Then reached high, tapping their brethren in the breeze. They were part of our woods then—until they rotted themselves hollow and fell.

3

LUCE

Waning Crescent (8% visible), Wednesday, October 14

MY MOM POURS Giblet's kibble into the bowl by the laundry room as I come down the stairs. She's still in the button-down pajamas and floral robe I bought her last Mother's Day. Her skin is shiny from her morning face cream and her hair is wound up in a silk scarf. I once had long hair like her, but I recently asked my mom to cut it into a blocky, asymmetrical bob—much to her dismay. Mine too, because so many people stared at me the next day.

"Morning," I say.

"Morning," her voice croaks. She pushes the button on her coffee machine. She always says she can't talk before caffeine. I prefer the silence anyway. I pop two pieces of bread into the toaster and stand at the sliding door that leads to our back porch, searching the trees. No eyes. The forest is far less menacing in the morning light. The trees wave happily, their leaves kissed yellow and orange.

The doorbell rings and Giblet hops around her bowl, barking as though an intruder will steal her breakfast. *She has the memory of a goldfish*, my mom likes to say. It's Anders at the door. Just like every morning.

I forget the woods, and force the toaster lever to deliver the toast early. The pieces are still a little pale, but I shuffle them onto paper towels and smear peanut butter on them. My mom pours a cup of coffee, stirs in a sugar cube, and blows on it before taking her first sip.

The doorbell rings again.

"Hold your horses," I shout, dropping the peanut butter knife into the sink.

"Neigh," he says, his voice muffled through the front door.

I roll my eyes, but can't help smiling too. My mom gives me a look until I pull the knife back out of the sink, swipe a sponge over it, and transfer it to the dishwasher. She crosses from the kitchen to the foyer, tightening the belt on her robe, and opens the door. "Good morning, Anders," she says, managing to sound more alive now that she's had coffee.

"Good morning, Miss Janice." The *Miss* is something his parents taught him to say. I have protested many times, because it sounds like he's talking to his preschool teacher instead of the mom who would smear chamomile on our welts when we returned from the forest covered in poison ivy.

I sling my backpack over my shoulder and hand him one of the slices on the paper towel.

"Yesss. Crunchy peanut butter." We take turns bringing breakfasts for each other, but I'm the better breakfast provider by far. He always has boiled eggs and fruit because his parents are health nuts.

"Bye," I say.

"Have a good day," my mom calls.

"You too," Anders says, skipping down the steps, his strides nearly double the length of my own. He would have been a basketball player if it weren't for the fact that he hates sports. It's all theater for him—both school performances and Picnic's community plays. Secretly, I think his talent is all in his thick mocha-colored eyebrows. They're the most expressive part of his face and, coupled with an angular jaw, the nearly black sweep of hair, and dimples, fill the seats of Picnic's barn theater with swooning old ladies.

There's no possibility of traffic, so he starts down the middle of our street. We love having the neighborhood all to ourselves. The subdivision was abandoned by the developers not long after they carved a half-moon into the woods, built two model homes, and poured a little concrete—sidewalks that start and stop, driveways that go nowhere, basements that sit like empty troughs—to make our quiet loop of a street. Our houses—the models sold off cheap after the work stalled— were finished with optimistic chrome light fixtures, hardwood floors, stone fireplaces, and plush carpeting. Picnic was full of optimism back before the railroad closed and people stopped moving to town.

Anders makes a big show of swallowing a chewy bite of toast. "You should have brought a glass of milk," he says, mouth still full.

"Oh, sorry, I'll go back."

I pretend I'm about to turn around, but he grabs my elbow lightly. My skin tingles under his fingers. This is also new territory for us. We've been friends for ages, but we aren't really the touchy-feely or cuddly types.

"When I get my car, we can carry milk in the cup holders," he says, gesturing with his free hand like he's conjuring a vision of the future. Anders's birthday is less than a week away, and we have been counting down until he has a license and we can skip the mile walk from our subdivision down the corn-lined country road to the Fitzgeralds' farm where the bus picks us up. Mostly, I can't wait to skip the bus entirely, which always smells like ham for some reason I don't care to investigate.

He drops his hand from my arm, but I can still feel the imprint of his fingers there. I want to look, but I resist the urge.

It grows warm as we walk, though the heat feels thin, as if it will end in a day or two. The sky is beginning its transformation from sharp summer blue to winter's slate gray, and the corn is drying out. It won't be long before the leaves in the trees behind our house have all fallen.

"So what's all this about eyes?" Anders asks.

"There was a pair of yellow eyes in the forest last night." The memory makes goose bumps rise on my arms again. "They just watched and watched our house and didn't move for a long time."

"Sounds like something straight out of a movie."

"A scary one," I say. Anders and I have a tradition of watching one scary movie a year, on Halloween. Well, he watches it, and I peek out from behind my fingers.

"Think it was an animal?" he asks.

I shrug. "Something big. I think I scared it away when I took out Giblet."

"Maybe a wolf?" he asks.

"There aren't wolves around here," I say.

"Sure, there are. In the sanctuary down south."

We went on a field trip to the sanctuary once, back in middle school. We sat on metal bleachers on the other side of a tall plexiglass wall from the wolves as the caretakers fed them raw hamburger and roadkill deer. At the end, we got to howl with them, starting with a quiet *Oooooo*, like we were the moaning ghosts at St. Anthony's, and getting louder until the wolves couldn't resist joining the chorus.

"Okay, fine. There aren't *wild* wolves around here," I say.

"One could have escaped."

"Doubt it. I feel like they would have mentioned it on the news with how little happens around here."

He points a finger into the air like he just thought of something. "You know how Mr. Kriska lives on the other side of the woods?"

I shake my head.

"Well, at play practice once, I remember him saying he had been watched by something at night."

"Mr. Kriska also thinks Bigfoot and the Loch Ness Monster are real," I say.

"Hey, be nice."

"I'm always nice!"

He laughs. Anders loves Mr. Kriska, our sophomore English teacher and the play director. But to most of the town, he's known to be a bit of a conspiracy nut with *one screw loose*. When he was a teen, he claimed to have spotted one of Picnic's Vila—the shape-shifting fairies that turn men into trees with their songs—and went on a crusade to hunt the monster, which, as far as the rumors go, is still ongoing.

Anders and I pass the fruit farm where we worked for a summer when we were thirteen, picking strawberries, blueberries, and raspberries for measly pocket change, and the haunted corn maze where we both worked last Halloween season. We were assigned the electric chair station. When maze-goers appeared, Anders sat on the chair, which lit up and made a loud buzzing sound. Ever the performer, he shook and yelled for effect. While the marks' attention was on him, I jumped out of the corn from behind. We got screams every time.

"We were the best ghoulish duo there ever was," he says, nodding toward the field.

Anders stops suddenly, his gaze trained on the cornfield, his thick brows knitted together like he is concentrating hard. "Hold up. Do you see them?"

"What?"

"Right there. Eyes."

I shiver despite the heat and scan the gold stalks. "Seriously? Can you tell what it is?" I ask.

He squints and shakes his head. "We'll flush it out." And just like that, Anders hops across the ditch and takes off running into the corn. "Come on!" he shouts over his shoulder.

"But the bus!" I call after.

I'm wearing my new shoes—the one pair I'm allotted before school starts each year—but Anders crashes through the stalks, whooping with a glee that is impossible to resist. I run after him, batting away the papery corn leaves and trying to follow his red tee.

Anders is too fast for me. I freeze, trying to listen for him, but he must have stopped somewhere too. The corn is almost silent, except for the soft whisper of leaves and flutter of tassels in the breeze. Like the night before, my skin crawls.

"Anders?"

Nothing.

"This isn't funny, Anders."

A few grackles rise from the corn, cawing like they are

incensed. Did Anders scare them? Or the predator? I make my way toward where they took off, my new shoes sinking into the damp soil.

"Boo!"

Something wraps around my middle from behind. I pry desperately at whatever has caught me, my heart hammering. But it's Anders's arm, of course.

The adrenaline makes my ears echo and skin tingle. It's another moment before I can speak. "You didn't even see the eyes, did you?"

He rests his chin on my shoulder. "Well, no, but . . ." he says softly, right into my ear. The hairs inside my ear feel like live wires, like I might jolt at the next sound. I am also acutely aware his arm is touching my fleshy middle, which I always try to hide with high-waisted pants and loose shirts. It's too much. I wriggle free.

"We're going to miss the bus," I say sharply, spinning toward the road and picking my way back through the stalks. He trots after me.

"Come on. You're terrible at pretending to be mad."

"I *am* mad."

"No, you're not." He shuffles so he is beside me, his nose not far from my jawbone. "Yeah, riiiiight . . . there. That's how I can tell." He points at my cheek. "That muscle kinda quivers when you're holding back a smile."

"You're making that up." And he probably is, but he's right

too; I *am* about to smile. It's hard not to with Anders around.

The smile breaks across my face.

"Gotcha," he says.

The bus drops us at the flagpole, where Ashleigh is waiting, perched on the brick flower boxes beside the sign that says *Picnic High School*. I assume she's doing her calculus homework, based on the way she's nervously chewing on the skin along her pinkie. Knowing her, it's probably homework that isn't due for days, but *it has to be perfect*—for her mom's sake more than hers.

Ashleigh is wearing jeans and a powder-blue shirt that probably came from the children's section. Considering she's 4'10", her options are limited. She compensates for the children's clothes with a face full of expertly done makeup and curled shiny blond hair.

"Hey, Ash," Anders says, pulling her into a half hug. I feel the heat rise in my neck. Maybe he's just becoming a touchier person all around?

Anders and Ashleigh grew close last year in marching band. Even though I became friends with Ashleigh too, I still feel a little like a third wheel when the three of us are together. Not that we hang out much outside of school. Most of the time, I'm helping my mom at the salon, or assisting her with weddings, or babysitting my cousin, Madison. Anders and Ashleigh are even busier. Anders plays the trumpet, takes voice lessons, and stars in every theater production. Ashleigh is a Mathlete, a cheerleader, and in band.

"That's wrong," Anders says, pointing at something on Ashleigh's page. She looks worried for a moment and then shakes her head vigorously.

"No, it's not." She's a year ahead of us in math, and Anders is an average student at best. She catches him trying to conceal his smile. "Wiseass."

She turns to me. "What's new with you?"

"Luce saw a wolf watching her," Anders says before I can reply.

"A wolf?" she asks.

"Shut it," I say. "Anders is trying to get me committed to St. Anthony's."

"Maybe you should talk to Mr. Kriska," Ashleigh says.

"That's what I said. Look at us, like two peas," Anders says. There it is again, that half hug.

The first bell rings and Anders leads us through the front doors, doling out *heys* to people he knows from band and theater. I watch to see if he touches anyone else. He doesn't, which leaves me even more confused. Maybe this new affection is only reserved for his best friends? Or did his arm around me, his mouth near my ear, mean something else?

Mr. Kriska sits at his desk, piled high with stacks of ungraded homework assignments. A white Styrofoam cup has left a brown ring on someone's vocabulary quiz and emits the smell of bitter teachers'-lounge coffee. Student-made posters plaster the walls—character maps for *Antigone* and plot diagrams for *The Odyssey*. Rather than taking them down when students turn in new ones, he tapes them over each other, so you could peel them away, counting years like the rings on a tree.

Mr. Kriska is staring out the window at the empty track, chin on his hand, one finger along his cheek, like he's lost in thought.

I never talk to teachers unless I absolutely have to—I hate the way it makes everyone look at you—but the room is still relatively empty, with only a few early birds settling into their seats.

"Mr. Kriska?"

He jumps a little and then peers over the narrow rectangles of his glasses at me. The skin on his hand looks translucent and is dotted with blue age spots. He has ears the size of Ashleigh's hands, a thick mustache that seems to sprout from his nose, flyaway wisps of white hair on his scalp, and eyebrows like fuzzy silver caterpillars. He's been a teacher for ages—he even taught my aunt and mom, and his own mother taught generations before that—but I've heard that the school administration is pushing him to retire. Vila rumors aside, he apparently forgets to submit attendance and grades, has fallen asleep during state testing, and even left a student in the bathroom on a field trip last year. I've seen him playing racquetball at the Y, though, and he can slam the ball against the wall with alarming power despite his sunken shoulders and humpback. He doesn't have to move much to win.

"Ms. Green," he says mildly.

I only have a minute or two before the rest of first period spills into the classroom. "I saw this weird thing last night in the woods, and Anders thought I should talk to you."

He sits up straight and scoots his chair closer to the desk. "What was it?" he asks.

"A pair of yellow eyes."

He glances around, like someone might be listening to us. More students have begun to trickle in, taking desks and dropping their backpacks to the floor. "Up high? In the branches?" he asks.

"No, closer to the ground. But not like a rodent. Bigger than that."

"Oh." He seems to lose interest and flips through a few papers on his desk as though searching for something.

"Anders said one time at practice you mentioned seeing something similar? That it was watching you?" I prompt.

He nods, locating a pen and notebook with a grid of blue lines where I see the names of my first-period class printed neatly. "A hawk or a falcon, I believe," he says. "Maybe an owl, but the eye shape didn't seem right."

"Oh, okay." I hitch my bag up, ready to find my seat at the back of the classroom.

But his eyes snap to me, sharp and bluish gray, piercing as

a winter sky. "Just tell me when you see them again," he says. His tone makes me feel jittery, like I chugged the whole cup of coffee on his desk. Why does he think the predator will come back?

4

LUCE

THAT NIGHT, THE yellow-gold eyes appear for the second time, shining steadily through the trees. It's my turn to wash the dishes, and my mom is on the couch watching TV, her head back against the cushion. She'll be softly snoring in no time.

I angle my neck so that the eyes line up with my own in the reflection. With my sharp bob and the animal's yellow-gold eyes, I can't help thinking I look fierce and powerful, like some character from a comic book. I kind of like it.

Giblet whines from the sliding glass door. "Luce, can you take her out?" my mom mumbles, her voice groggy. I glance at the eyes again; the hairs on the back of my neck rise.

Tell me when you see them again, Mr. Kriska said. If they were dangerous, he would have told me to stay away, right? Giblet and I were outside yesterday and nothing happened.

I dry my hands on a towel and text Anders.

They're out there again.

He texts back the eyeballs emoji.

Still don't see them?

Nope.

I flip off the light above the sink, hoping I will be better able to make out their shape or size so I can report back to Mr. Kriska.

Giblet whines again, starting to pace back and forth in front of the glass.

"Luce," my mom says.

"I'm going, I'm going."

I clip her leash on and stand on the back steps while she pees, safe in the bright cone of our floodlights. What do we look like to the predator, I wonder. A round white dog and an equally round white girl, spotlit and on display?

"What are you?" I call, hoping I sound less scared than I probably do.

Giblet glances at me before returning to the important business of snuffling in the grass. The eyes don't move.

I cup my hand around my mouth, remembering how I learned to howl at the wolf sanctuary. "Oooooooooooo," I call softly.

Giblet plops her butt in the grass and tilts her head to the side as though asking me a question. "Oooooooooooo," I ghost-moan. Then louder: "Ooooooooooo."

I am about to try full volume when my mom slides open the door, and I stop mid-howl. Her forehead is furrowed, the skin making a neat V between her eyebrows. "What are you doing?" she asks sharply.

"Howling."

"I can hear that, but why?"

Before I can answer, we hear a long, mournful *Aroooooooooo* from the woods. The howl sounds like it's coming from the place where I saw the creature. I scan the trees, but I can't find the yellow eyes anymore. They must be closed, the animal's throat open to the sky.

Arrooooooooooo. The howl is thin and reedy. Almost lonely. I hear more howls then—distant, like echoes. The animal closest to us seems to gain strength from its comrades, adding syllables to its call. *Aroooo-a-a-aroooooo.*

A few coyotes somewhere to the east join the fracas, their howls higher-pitched and interspersed with sharp yips.

That gets Giblet growling. A soft, under-the-breath *errrrrr.* "You tell 'em," I say.

My phone chimes. **Is that what I think it is?**

I text Anders back the wolf emoji.

"Luce, come inside." My mom's fists ball against her thighs. She reluctantly allowed Anders and me to play in the forest as kids—we wore her down with our begging and promises to respond as soon as she called to us. I have never once seen her

25

set foot in the woods herself, despite it being yards from our house. Maybe she's afraid, like so many other Picnickers?

"It's only wolves," I say happily, glad to have solved one part of the mystery. Still, I'm not sure why they're here.

Mom shakes her head like I am being naive. "They're wild animals, Luce," she says. She pulls me inside and slides the door shut. I can still hear them, though, their voices made softer and all the more haunting by the glass barrier between us.

5

FANYA

THE HOWL WITH the Girl and my Pack was the perfect start to the Big Hunt. Now it is time to run and sneak and carry. I pick Gray Form because it is strong in haunch, foot, and jaw, and my truest Form. Air Form is faster with its *fwup-fwup-fwup*ping wings, but its sharp eyes aren't good in the dark. Earth Form moves quiet through the grass and leaves and strikes prey to death, but it is too slow and weak for this hunt.

People Form is the least suited for any hunt, we all agree. Thick tongue. Smush face. Weak eyes. Weaker nose. Fingers? But People Form is the only one that can't be trapped. My ears flatten at the thought of being chained until Gone Forever. That is why I must hunt. The Old Ones say our Pack was once large, until the first trapping in the Old World, and then the second trapping here.

I leave the People Only Dens behind and run through the trees, remembering how Danica taught me to chase deer, her *huh-huh-huh*ing breaths matching my own, our eyes locked on the white of the prey's tail, the leaves hissing above us like Earth Forms. But of course, I am alone for this.

I smell an owl somewhere above me, a beaver not far upstream, and all the skittering, delicious mice. The small prey who love the yellow light are hiding in their nests, their tiny hearts *tick-tick-tick*ing.

I cross a cornfield and another after that. I weave between stalks and dart down long rows, the leaves brushing my shoulders. I flush a doe from where she hid in the corn, baring my teeth with a bark as she springs high, but I don't chase. I am not here for her.

At the edge of the cornfield, I come to the gray river that is hard like rocks beneath my toe pads. I run along the white lines until two lights swing toward me and force me back into the corn. A Night Beast charges down the hard river, roaring. It has round light-eyes, a flat humpback, and a broad nose. I crouch and growl, but it races by, ignoring me. I stick to the valley beside the gray river then, hiding each time a Night Beast tears past.

When I finally see the green Den for People Only with the caged-in grass patch and the lone tree that Old One Zora showed me in Air Form above, I swish my tail.

In the Old World, when the moon opened its eye wide for Forefathers' Eve, the Hunt was chosen because there were gifts of fine cloth, promises to be kept, and unwanted young. But

Zora picked this Den because it stands alone instead of in rows with other Dens for People Only, because the top-floor glass is easy to slide open with a beak, because the prey inside is still small.

I can see the blue of a light box through the front glass and a fox-furred People Only folding cloth. I smell charred cow and spring onions.

I sneak forward, slow-pawed and steady. Above, there is the glass Zora showed me, a dim light inside and something hanging and spinning slow.

To reach the top glass, I heart-decide to be Air and feel the feathers tickle down my spine. My back paws curl tightly into talons. My front paws grow long and light-boned, my nose sharp and hard. It aches to change, like my Form doesn't want to let go of Gray, but I also feel strong and new.

It's time to begin, Old One Teodora said before I left the Den.

I stretch my wings and take off.

OUR HOME

OUR HOME IN the old world had many names. Many kings and queens who claimed to rule it. Many lines drawn on the mossy floor. We didn't concern ourselves with the affairs of men. Our concerns were the bison: that they remained fat and plentiful. The trees: that they were dense and tall. The streams: that they were clear and cool. The winter: that it was merciful.

What are you? Where do you come from? we were asked from time to time.

We are what was created by the gods long, long ago to protect the woods. The first of our kind—four orphaned sisters—were given the powers and knowledge to make others in their likeness. Only under the full moon that falls on Forefathers' Eve, when the boundary between the gods' world and ours is at its thinnest, the magic strongest, can we add another sister to our pack.

6

LUCE

Waning Crescent (3% visible), Thursday, October 15

I AM ASLEEP when I hear my mom's cell phone ring on the other side of the wall. The only other time someone called this late was when my grandma fell on a riverboat casino and broke her hip. I push myself up on my elbows and try to listen. I can hear my mom's voice, low at first, and then high and fast. A cold sweat prickles at my hairline. Something has happened.

A few moments later, the light turns on outside my door. My mom knocks softly.

"Luce?"

"Yeah?" I rub my eyes as light from the hallway spills inside.

"That was Cindy. Madison is missing."

"Missing?" My brain is still sleep-fuzzed. Missing as in disappeared? As in got lost? As in ran off? As in taken?

No, that can't be. My cousin, Madison, is two and a half. I

31

babysit her while my aunt works weekends or goes on dates. She giggles at my Grover and Cookie Monster impressions. She insists on water with exactly four ice cubes before bed as a stalling tactic. She likes to bite cucumbers like bananas and push a plastic lawn mower across the carpeting. How can a little red-headed toddling thing with rolls at her wrists go missing?

"I'm going to wait with Cindy while the police search," Mom says. Cindy has a different mother and was born when my mom was already a teenager—but they're super close and cut hair side by side every day.

"Should I come? I might be able to help." I know all Madison's hiding spots: the laundry basket in Cindy's closet, the cabinet beside the Crock-Pot, the living room curtains. A lump forms in my throat. How can she be gone?

"No. You have school tomorrow," my mom says. "I'll call your grandma and drop you there for the rest of the night."

"Mom, I'll be fine by myself," I say. "I'm fifteen. Plus, you don't have time to drive me a half hour to Gran's. You need to go now."

She hesitates a moment, biting her nails, and then nods. "I'll have my cell and I'll call you in the morning if I'm not back."

I am too busy worrying about Madison to be surprised Mom agreed to this plan. "Tell Cindy—" But I can't come up with something to say. All I can think about is how I watched my aunt at the salon when she was pregnant, gently bumping her belly against her clients as she leaned over them to cut their hair. *Oh, pardon*, she'd say sweetly, but not at all like she was sorry. I love that about her.

I try to swallow away the heaviness in my throat. I don't want to cry and give my mom something else to worry about. Cindy needs her more than I do.

"Luce—keep the doors locked, okay?"

That sends a bolt of terror through me, leaving my skin clammy. Picnic isn't the kind of place where people lock their doors, especially not out in the country where we live.

When the garage door groans closed, I climb out of bed and lift one of the slats of my blinds, wondering if the eyes will be there again. I stare into the trees, but the moon is behind a cloud, and all I can see are the shifting masses of leaves—like crushed velvet against the navy sky.

7

FANYA

I TRY TO sleep through yellow light. The Earth Forms go to rest on their rocks in the sunbeams. The Airs dip and dive for songbirds. I am with the other Grays—Danica, Alina, Nina—tangled with their tails and paws.

"Waaaaaaahhhhh."

I stretch and groan. Old One Teodora has made a cage for the prey, driving tall sticks into the dirt. The small People Only stands inside, one hand wrapped around a stick. Another smashed into her mouth. She is the size of a badger with a fox's red fur on her head and puffed cheeks, shiny from eye-water.

"Waaaaaaaaahhhhhh," she wails again. Other Grays groan. Old One Nina stretches her white forelegs, rolls out her long tongue, and then tucks her snout under her tail. The Small wailed all dark too, stopping only at pink light to sleep fitfully, rolling from back to stomach and whimpering softly.

I circle-pace around her cage. After picking her up and carrying her back here, I know not to get too close. Those fingers pinch. And she bites.

"Waaaaahhhhh." She shakes the sticks and stomps her fuzzy blue feet at me. Maybe she wants food?

I belly crawl out of the Den and blink away the bright yellow light. I heart-decide Air and coast above the trees, over the fields, until I spot a brown bird that hasn't seen my shadow. It flits here and there like it doesn't know which way to go, chittering happily. Then it glides, preparing to land on a tree branch. My cue to plunge. My Form flattens, my feet tuck, my wings become rigid. The air is fast and hard against my face.

I carry it back to our clearing and scuttle beneath Great Tree. I hop to the cage and drop it just outside the sticks. My talons have done their job. The bird is still, Gone Forever.

"Eat," I say, but it comes out *Err-err*.

The fox-furred Small jumps back and looks at me with blue eyes as round as an owl's. I nudge the sparrow into the cage with my beak. The Small shrinks even farther away, balling her fists against her cheeks.

"I don't want!" she shouts.

I tilt my head. What could the Small want if not food?

"Where is Maa-mmmaaaa?" she sobs.

Maa-mmmaaaa. What is that?

"Where is Mama?" she says again. Does she mean the larger fox-furred People Only folding cloth in the green Den for

People? The People Only that Zora told me to sneak and hide from once I got inside—was that *Mama*?

Teodora crawls into the Den in People Form. She holds more vines and sticks for the cage.

I heart-decide People too, my feathers thinning until they are a light dust on my skin, my body and toes and fingers stretching, my nose softening and dulling. My eyes grow dimmer and foggier too, but new colors appear. I push to standing on my naked fish feet.

"The Small cries for Mama," I say. "What is Mama?"

"It means Mother," Teodora says. She tries to use her People fingers to tie the vines, but is clumsy. She drops the vines, shakes out her hands, and then picks them up again.

"Mother?"

Teodora sticks out her tongue and manages to pull a knot tight. "A Mother helps a Small grow. Teaches it to eat and talk and survive."

But Danica taught me to hunt as Gray. To crouch and wait. To tire the prey and tackle. Then to tear and eat.

I look at the Small, who has shoved her fingers back in her mouth and is whimpering again. If I took this Small from her Mother—will it be my job to teach her to be one of us?

8

LUCE

WHEN MY ALARM goes off in the morning, I have to scrape my eyelids open. I lay in bed for hours after the phone call, listening for my mom to come home, which would surely signal that Madison had been found safe. I must have fallen asleep eventually, but it was the kind of sleep where you feverishly slip in and out of dreams. In one, I heard my cousin laugh in the forest. I tried to find her, but no matter how fast I ran, she always seemed far away. The worst part was that I heard twigs cracking a few steps behind me. Every time I spun around, I couldn't see anything. But I could feel someone—or something—following me.

Downstairs, the kitchen is empty, my mom's coffee pot silent and cold. Giblet springs from her bed, her whole body wiggling with the movement of her tail.

"Oh, I bet you have to pee," I say, sliding open the door to let her out.

There's no breeze; the trees are still. I cross the lawn and stand right at the woods' edge. I can see the forest floor, matted with decomposing leaves, for a few feet, and then the light fades. Could there be something waiting in the shadows?

Giblet barks, a high yip that means she's hungry. I walk backward from the forest, keeping my eye on it all the way back to the house. Inside, I pour kibble into Giblet's bowl and flip on the TV.

A red banner scrolls across the screen: *Amber Alert, 2-year-old Madison Green, last seen Picnic, Illinois.* The channel displays the photo Cindy keeps on the side table in her living room: Madison's hair is in pigtails and she's holding a stuffed yellow duck to her chest.

"... went missing from her house in Picnic, Illinois, between the hours of seven and eleven yesterday evening," the anchor says, his face arranged in what I imagine is supposed to read as deep concern. "She was last seen wearing blue footed pajamas. Local search parties will commence this morning. Anyone with information is encouraged to call the tip line below."

I can picture the pajamas he's talking about—a fuzzy onesie with a brown bear stitched on the chest that Madison would pull into her mouth and suck on. I feel the pressure of tears behind the bridge of my nose. My mind spins.

Images flash: Madison, confused and alone somewhere, unable to ask for help.

Madison, kept in a tiny room, never allowed to grow into

the smiley, happy kid that I know she will be.

Madison, gone. Disappeared. Forever.

I shake my head to clear away the thoughts.

Maybe my mom is home and has simply overslept. Maybe Madison is back, already in her booster seat at the kitchen table eating Cheerios and blueberries with her fingers and chattering about wanting to be a kitty cat for Halloween and going trick-or-treating for the first time.

Or maybe—

My cell phone rings before I allow myself to complete the thought.

"Morning, Luce." Mom sounds tired, her voice gravelly. I wish I could see her face so I'd know how to feel. "Is everything okay?" she asks.

"Just watching the news. They haven't found her yet?" I ask.

"No," she says quietly.

"How's Cindy?"

My mom inhales, a long sound that I take to mean *terrible*.

"What happened? Can you say?" I ask—both wanting and not wanting the answer at the same time.

"One minute."

I can hear my mom's breath huffing like she's climbing stairs. I imagine her at Cindy's, going into one of the bedrooms to talk privately. Maybe even Madison's, standing on the rug decorated with bright red-and-blue galaxies, beneath the star mobile that spins from the ceiling. Or maybe she can't go in—

maybe the police have it closed off. Do they do that when a child goes missing?

A moment later, my mom continues: "Cindy put her down to bed like usual. She went back to check on her a few hours later and the crib was empty."

"Someone broke in?"

"The window in Madison's room doesn't latch and they found the kitchen door unlocked, though Cindy swears she locked it. She was downstairs the entire time watching TV and folding laundry."

I glance around, like the thing that had been following me in my dream might be in our house, but the whole kitchen is sunlit and warm, the white granite countertops glittering.

The doorbell rings and I jump. Giblet pounces out of her bed, letting out a high-pitched string of barks.

"That Anders?" my mom asks, as though it could be someone else.

I look around the corner to the foyer. Anders's dark flop of hair is visible through the door's frosted glass. "Yep," I say.

"I'll let you go, then. Straight to school and back right after, you hear?"

Normally, I would roll my eyes at my mom's overprotectiveness, but I don't today. "Are you sure I shouldn't stay home and wait to hear from you?" I do not want to face school on a day like this.

"Positive."

"Okay."

"Love you, Luce."

I swallow. "Love you."

We don't say the words often—not that she doesn't love me or vice versa. It just isn't part of our routine. Maybe she says it today because Madison's disappearance reminds her how fragile our time together is.

I think of Cindy leaning over the crib to kiss Madison's sleeping forehead when she returns from dates. Of her finding that same crib empty.

The doorbell rings again, eliciting more *arfs* out of Giblet. I can't find it in myself to yell *hold your horses*.

I swing open the door.

"Hiya" Anders says with a toss of his hair.

I stare back at him. Does he not know about Madison? His parents aren't fans of the news and opt out of alerts, but, in this town, they still should have heard by now.

"What? No breakfast?"

For some reason, that's the moment the tears break, in a wave so strong I can't catch my breath. I'm not even sure if I walk into his arms or if he steps forward to wrap them around me.

"What's wrong, Luce? What happened?"

"My—cousin—went—missing—last—night," I say between gasps.

"Oh shit. Madison?"

I manage to nod into his chest. I can feel his heart beating, and the steadiness of it calms me a little. "My mom went over to Cindy's last night. She's still there."

"Do you think she could have wandered off?" he asks. "Like, she could walk, right?"

I back out of the hug so I can see his face and palm the tears off my cheek. "Yeah, but I doubt that she could have gotten out of her crib and down the stairs without my aunt noticing. And then she'd have to get far enough away that police searching couldn't find her."

"I guess, but the alternative wouldn't happen in Picnic. Like, Luce, this is Pic-nic," Anders says, emphasizing both syllables of the name.

I nod, a little relieved by his confidence that the terrible scenarios I imagined earlier aren't possible. Picnic just isn't one of those places. Part of it is the small size; nothing ever happens. But another part is that everyone knows each other. Like, *knows* knows. Flaws, failings, all of it. You aren't going to get away with anything. Unless . . .

"What if it was a kidnapper from outside of town?" I ask.

"Someone would have seen them, then."

He is right about that too. Nothing gets by Picnic's watchers: the gray-haired ladies on their wraparound porches, the grizzled men leaning over their truck steering wheels.

I gather my things and lock up the house. We start down our street and turn onto the country road to pass the cornfields.

"Who's Madison's dad again?" Anders asks.

"Roald Turner."

Anders whistles. "Sucks to be him. The police will track him down."

I stop and stare at him. "Why do you think that?"

He shrugs. "Seems logical."

Madison's dad runs the register in his parents' butcher shop, where he apparently picks up all the women in his age bracket. At least that's what the ladies in the salon say. He is always sitting on the stool in front of the register, drumming on the counter like he needs to get the energy out of his body somehow. If I'd been a decade younger, people would say he was my dad too. But—to the great disappointment of the gossips in town—my mom is a single mom by choice, my biological father an anonymous donor.

"I thought you said it couldn't be a kidnapping," I say.

"Yeah." He flushes a little—enough to make me wonder if he'd just said that earlier to make me feel better. "But the police will definitely investigate the possibility."

Tears spring to my eyes again. Because if they go for Roald, they'll definitely come for Cindy too. She was the one home with Madison.

"Hey, hey," Anders says, grabbing me by the elbows and steering me so I'm facing him.

"They'll think it's my aunt, won't they?" I blubber.

Since sixth grade, I've been going to the salon after school to help sweep up and wash towels while my mom finishes with clients. Cindy makes sure the hot cocoa packets by the coffee machine are stocked for me. And if she has time, she practices updos on me—or she did before I chopped off my hair. I used to love the gentle tugs of her fingers on my scalp and watching her reflection, bobby pins pinched in her lips, fiery red hair straightened impeccably. *You're a picture*, she always said when she was done. Not *pretty as*. With her, it was about being a moment in time, something special, captured forever. How could anyone think someone so gentle and kind would do something to her own daughter?

"No way," Anders says, his thick eyebrows pinched together, his dark eyes locked on mine.

"Oh no? Remember, this is Pic-nic." I say it like Anders did earlier, emphasizing the syllables. Meaning, if Mr. Kriska's monster-sighting reputation stuck from the time he was a teenager, there is no way Cindy will escape this. I've heard enough passive-aggressive comments in the salon to understand that Picnickers already consider her *loose* just because she isn't married to Roald. It won't be a leap for them to start calling her a murderer too. Madison has to come back. She *has* to.

I feel like a boulder about to tumble downhill and there's no one to catch me—not even Anders.

Ashleigh is waiting for us at the flagpole, tugging her ponytail over her shoulder and furiously combing it with her fingers. Before we even descend the stairs, she calls, "Luce, are you okay?"

Everyone milling on the sidewalk turns to look at me, and I feel as though their gazes stick to my skin like tree sap. I shake my head at her, fighting back the tears that spring to my eyes again. I don't want even more people to look at me. Why did my mom make me go to school today?

"They'll find her," Anders says from behind me like it isn't even a question. I swallow and nod stiffly.

Ashleigh links her elbow in mine. "Let's go inside," she says.

It's even worse inside. Not only can I feel the eyes, I can hear the whispers. My cousin's name over and over. And my aunt's too. My cheeks, neck, and chest feel hot, likely splotched with the red patches I get when I'm upset or nervous.

Ashleigh steers me to my locker, Anders turns my combination for me, and then they both take me to English—even though it's still before first bell.

"Mr. Kriska will let us wait in his room," Anders says. Mr. Kriska's room is a sanctuary not only for the actors and set crew, but also for outsiders who are bullied and need a place to eat lunch, or the kids who don't want to go home and stay after school to clean his room and organize his papers. The fact that he's an outsider too seems to draw them there.

His room is empty when we arrive. He's at the chalkboard, fists ground into the back of his hips, a piece of chalk in one hand that has left dust all over his khakis. He seems to be deciding what to write—or pondering what is already there: *reading quiz*. The knot of dread in my stomach for Madison and

45

Cindy grows tighter. I'm a terrible quiz- and test-taker—even though I study and do all my homework. It's like there's some switch in my brain that turns off my memory when I'm nervous, and the fact that I can't remember makes me anxious. So it's a loop I can't seem to escape. Cindy has been coaching me in meditation—deep breaths in and out—so that I can stay calm. I try one now, breathing in through my nose, holding it for a few counts, and releasing it slowly. I feel a little better.

"Mr. Kriska, do you mind if we hang out in here until the bell?" Anders asks.

"Not at all—" His eyes catch on mine a moment too long.

"Her cousin is missing," Ashleigh says, as though there could be any other reason he'd be staring.

"I heard. I'm terribly sorry." He gestures at an empty desk at the front.

I sit down, but immediately feel trapped by the armrest and stand again. I hug myself instead. If I close my eyes, I see Madison, nose pressed to the glass panes of her front window and making *er-roo-er-roo* sounds like a fire truck. I try to deep breathe again, but it sounds like a groan.

"Ms. Green, did you see them again?" he asks. "The eyes?"

I'm thrown by this. What do the eyes have to do with my cousin? "Uh . . . yeah," I say. The memory of howling with the creature feels distant, like something that happened years ago instead of last night.

"How did the intruder get into your cousin's house, if you

don't mind me asking?" He's looking at me through the lenses of his glasses, so his eyes appear magnified and bright.

"Maybe the kitchen door, though my aunt swears it was locked. Or the bedroom window. It didn't latch."

"Up high?"

I feel goose bumps at the repetition of that question, the same one he asked me yesterday. "The second story," I answer, wary now. Is he going to blame Vila and Bigfoot?

His eyes go wide. "Not again."

"Again?" Anders repeats.

Mr. Kriska slides open one of his desk drawers and pulls out a stapler and a pile of papers. He digs and shuffles a bit more, then withdraws a slim leather-bound book. The words *Picnic's Promise* are embossed on the brown leather, with *Anton Kriska* in a cursive typeface below.

"Not me. My grandfather," he says, as though he can tell I'm wondering about the name. I've heard that the conspiracy-nut gene was passed down through the men in his family, and his father—and his father before him—were just as strange. "He's the reason I love the theater." He hands the book to me.

"What is it?" Ashleigh asks as I flip open to the first page. There's a list of characters followed by a script.

I glance at Mr. Kriska. "Read it," he says.

I begin to read, Anders and Ashleigh leaning over my shoulders.

PICNIC'S PROMISE
ACT ONE
Scene One
Picnic, Illinois, 1868

THOMAS, dressed in worn but carefully patched clothing, stokes the fire in the stove restlessly. CATHERINE, wearing a similarly worn blouse and skirt, is kneading dough at the table. A portrait of Thomas in a Union Civil War uniform hangs on the wall. There is a woodstove, a small table, and two chairs. In the next room, there is a cradle, a rocking chair, and a bed. Otherwise, the rooms are bare. Rain is heard outside and gray light spills through the single window.

CATHERINE

You cannot convince the corn to dry by harassing the fire, Tom.

THOMAS stops stoking the fire.

THOMAS

I cannot sit idly by while my family starves either. We shall have nothing in our stores for winter if it doesn't stop raining.

CATHERINE

My father will give you a position at the grocery. I have told you this.

THOMAS

At what cost though? I shall lose all respect.
Especially my own.

CATHERINE

No one will blame you for taking a hand. The
rebellion was hard on us all.

THOMAS

Except your father.

CATHERINE stops kneading. THOMAS stands and paces.

CATHERINE

I'll admit our family has been lucky, but he
gave generously to support the soldiers and to
those who remained behind in Picnic. He sent
all his sons and his only son-in-law to fight the
rebels.

THOMAS

Sent us? You know he would have tried to pay
the commutation fees if we hadn't volunteered.

THOMAS grows alert and stares at the next room where the crib is.

Martha usually wakes to eat by now.

CATHERINE

Rouse her.

THOMAS goes into the next room. He lifts the blankets. The crib is empty.

THOMAS

Catherine! She's gone.

CATHERINE stands and rushes into the next room. She searches the crib as well.

CATHERINE

Where is my baby?

THOMAS

How could someone have snuck in? We were
here the whole time! Who would do such a thing?

CATHERINE

Where is my baby?

Wails.

I look up from the page. "What is this?" My voice is hoarse.
Anders gently touches my back.

"Just keep reading," Mr. Kriska says.

ACT ONE
Scene Two

THOMAS sits in a chair, head in hands. CATHERINE paces, clutching the crib blanket to her chest. Two older men stand in the room, CONSTABLE COLLINS and MAYOR WELLS. The CONSTABLE wears a vest and watch chain. The MAYOR wears a frock coat, low-cut vest, and a cravat tied in a bow.

CONSTABLE COLLINS

The child made no noise?

CATHERINE

None at all, sir.

CONSTABLE COLLINS

And what time was it that you put her to bed?

CATHERINE

It was after supper. The sun hadn't set.

CONSTABLE COLLINS

And you were both in the house the entire time?

CATHERINE

(*exasperated*) Yes! Right outside the room. We would have heard something if someone took her.

CONSTABLE COLLINS

(*to THOMAS*) Mrs. White said she saw you in the cemetery the night before last.

THOMAS *lifts his head.*

She said you had a tree branch and were charging a stone like it was an opponent.

THOMAS

My nightmares are nothing new to the gossips of Picnic. They can't keep their tongues from wagging.

CONSTABLE COLLINS

Many of our returned soldiers have nightmares, Thomas. Few take them to the streets.

CATHERINE

What are you saying? (*to MAYOR WELLS*) What is he saying, Father?

THOMAS

I understand the meaning, Catherine. Picnic
always finds a way to turn on its own.

MAYOR WELLS

Clears his throat.

That's enough for tonight, Constable. Don't
you agree? Let's get a search party going.

*CONSTABLE COLLINS nods, but continues to watch THOMAS, who has
dropped his head.*

The first bell rings before I can read more. Ashleigh hitches
her backpack onto her shoulder and glances at the door, probably worried about the tardy bell even though we have ten
minutes.

"Wait, so this really happened?" Anders asks.

"Happens," Mr. Kriska corrects. I stare at the man and his
twitching mustache. Madison is gone, and he gave me a play,
written by his grandfather, about a little girl who went missing
in the 1800s and the town blaming a parent.

My hands are shaking, and I realize that they're all looking at me. The boulder is picking up speed again, downhill,
fast and furious. "My cousin is missing," I say, my voice low,
catching in the back of my throat. "There's no time for fiction

53

or conspiracy theories or . . . whatever this is." I toss the script onto Mr. Kriska's desk. "There's no time for any of this." I gesture at the chalkboard, the stacks of papers, the whole school.

I'm out the door then, my vision sparking. I'm dimly aware of Anders's voice, echoing in my ears, but I can't make out the words.

9

LUCE

I DON'T KNOW where I am or where I'm going until I'm outside the school. I drop onto the curb and take a few breaths. The world becomes clear around me again: the brick flower boxes with their orange and pink mums, the flagpole creaking as the wind tugs the flag, students jogging across the parking lot before the tardy bell, Anders and Ashleigh sinking onto the curb beside me.

"Luce, maybe you should go to the nurse. She'll probably let you lie down on the cot," Ashleigh says.

"No way. I'm not going back in there with all those—" *eyes*, I finish in my head.

"Where will you go?" Anders asks.

"They said on the news that there's a search party," I say. I ignore the fact that the characters in Mr. Kriska's ridiculous play suggested the same thing. "I can't just do nothing at school all day."

I push myself to my feet and rub the gravel off my palms.

"Are you coming?" I ask.

Anders and Ashleigh glance at each other. "My mom will kill me if I skip," Ashleigh says. I don't blame her; I've met her mom, a former Miss Picnic who runs the Women's Club in town, an invite-only group that does nothing but plan charity socials. She's the reason Ashleigh can't bear to make a mistake on her math homework or be tardy to class.

I raise my eyebrows at Anders. "How will you get there?" he asks.

"Walk," I say, even though Cindy's house is well over two miles outside town.

Anders's brows shoot up. His dark eyes search my face as though for some answer to a question I haven't asked. "We better get started," he says. "Cover for us, Ash."

"How?"

"You're a smartie, you'll figure it out."

I feel a swell of warmth inside that tunnels through the worry and fear.

The search party is easy to spot, their cars lining the country road that crosses Cindy's street. Her green two-story house sits on a small parcel of land surrounded by farms—sold off, I'm sure, when the railroad closed.

A fiftysomething woman I presume to be the party leader stands with her boot toe on the bumper of a car, a map unfolded on the hood. I recognize her from the salon. Her thick forearms are often smeared with dried frosting and streaked with food coloring. I think she runs a custom-cake business, but now she looks more like a construction worker than a baker, in heavy boots, a neon safety vest, and a headlight that seems unnecessary in the bright fall sun.

She doesn't seem to recognize me. She points to a spot on her map—neatly gridded with red marker—and tells us to find our team there, in a square of woods beyond the farms, not far from the Picnic campground.

"Stick together. You know how these woods can be," the woman tells us, her eyes darting suspiciously in their direction. "Keep your eyes peeled for blue."

I picture Madison in those pajamas when I babysat a few weeks ago, pulling books off her shelf and dragging them to the chair in the corner of her room so I could read to her before bed.

Anders places his hand firmly between my shoulder blades. "Thanks," he says, moving us away from the woman.

We cross a farmer's land, walking on a mowed path between a cornfield and a bean field, and step into the forest. The temperature drops almost immediately, and the air feels damper too. I'm transported to the summers Anders and I spent hidden from the sun under the canopy, marching down gullies with walking sticks that could transform into wizard staffs or lances.

Somehow, as we've aged, the forest has become more

impenetrable—or we've lost the ability to navigate it as easily as we once could. We try to stay in a straight line, moving toward the calls of "Madison!" But the ground between the trees is a mess of bramble bushes and fallen tree branches. We pick our way around a patch of poison ivy, but have to step into twisted brush with pliable twig-like branches that wrap around our ankles and thorns that grab at our jeans and hair.

I step over a log and right into a spiderweb. I make a sputtering sound and paw at my face.

"What? What happened?" Anders asks, then gives a small smile and peels some of it off my cheek. "We are going to have to do a very thorough tick check after this."

The thought of his long fingers searching my skin for ticks makes my temperature rise a few degrees. I push up my sleeves and shake away the thought. Madison is missing and that's all my brain can process right now.

"Think there are any snakes?" Anders asks. He's been afraid of them since we were kids, even though we've never spotted anything more than a garter snake.

"Oh, most definitely," I say.

He shoots me an exaggerated glare, and I can't help smiling back.

We find the party—ten people, mostly gray-haired in vests and gardening gloves—moving in a line across the campground. The campground itself—a patch of grass with fire rings and dirt driveways where campers can park—is empty. There aren't a lot of midweek off-season campers.

"Mitzi didn't have any more vests and gloves?" a man with a pair of binoculars around his neck asks us.

I shake my head, assuming Mitzi is the cake baker. The man looks at our shoes—not the boots we should have worn, apparently—and sighs. He beckons us to the line and points to the end. "Stay within arm's length and don't touch anything that you find."

Anders and I fall into place next to an elementary school crossing guard, who is wearing her crossing vest over camo coveralls—as though she can't decide whether she wants to be visible or hidden. She greets us with a tight smile, and we march forward slowly at her side, stooping to inspect bits of trash stuck in the grass to see if anything hints at Madison's whereabouts. Unfortunately, the Hershey's candy bar wrappers and empty Hebrew National packaging don't tell us anything.

Still, it feels a little better to be doing something besides sitting in school wondering if I'll hear my name over the inter-com, called to the office because of some terrible update.

"Madison!" I yell.

The sound echoes against the dense forest.

Anders's pocket buzzes and mine chimes. We both pull out our phones, even though the crossing guard clears her throat meaningfully. "You gotta keep your eyes peeled," she says, repeating Mitzi.

Anders smiles, charmingly, of course, and looks down at his phone anyway. It's Ashleigh, texting our group thread.

The police are here! Detectives, I think.

I look at Anders, who runs a hand through his hair, eyebrows practically to his hairline.

They're talking to Mr. Kriska in the guidance counselor's office.

"No shit!" Anders says, texting a bunch of exclamation points back to Ashleigh. "They can't think Mr. Kriska is involved. Right?"

Our line finishes the campground and enters the woods on the other side. I push aside a branch with sharp thorns, wishing I had gardening gloves.

"You read that play too. It was creepy. More than creepy," I say. I regret giving it back. If the police think Mr. Kriska knows something, maybe the play would have provided a clue as to where Madison is.

"But it's Mr. Kriska." He tosses his head, and I see dampness along his sideburns. His collar is damp too. With the time it took us to walk here, we've already been outside for hours.

I try to move a branch that's at abdomen height, but can't and have to duck under it instead. I keep my eyes on the ground, but everything is shades of brown. "He clearly knows something," I say. "You heard him say this *happens*. Present tense."

"I know, but come on. If someone had disappeared in Picnic before, we would have heard about it."

I'm not as sure about that. My mom always says Picnic knows everyone's business but that the town has its secrets too. I turn to the crossing guard, who is windmilling her arms slowly—either stretching her shoulders or clearing away obstacles. "Have you heard of a disappearance like this before?" I ask her.

"Oh yes," she says immediately. "Gosh, how many years ago. Twenty? She came back the next day like nothing happened, though."

"See?" Anders says, as if what the crossing guard said somehow proved his point instead of mine.

"What was her name?" I ask the woman.

"*R-a*-something. Raquel or Raegan maybe. The parents got divorced not long after it happened. The father took the daughter and moved south, I think, after the railroad closed."

"Really? Wow. So, why do you think we haven't heard this before?" I ask.

"Well, she was found, wasn't she? And the mother—" She shakes her head. "She wasn't the sharpest. I wonder if the girl was even missing at all."

I want to search on my phone to see if I can find anything about a missing girl, but my hands are too occupied with keeping me upright and free of scratches.

So this *has* happened before, like Mr. Kriska said, and the girl reappeared. I can hold on to that.

When I get home later, I let Giblet out and head straight to the shower. My cheeks are streaked from sweat and dirt, and I can see the line on my collarbone where my shirt covered my chest. All that dirt despite the fact that we found nothing, and, eventually, Anders and I had to hike back to town so that we could catch the bus home.

Before the buses arrived, we saw Ashleigh briefly, and she filled us in on calling the school and pretending to be our moms, as well as the fact that Mr. Kriska was gone by the time she had English. I wonder if that means they're closer to finding Madison.

My mom dashes those hopes when I get out of the shower. **No news,** she texts. **Make yourself something to eat. I'm staying here with Cindy a bit longer.**

I stain-treat my white shoes and throw my clothes into the washer to soak before making a pot of mac and cheese and settling onto the couch to eat. Giblet curls up in my lap, and I use her side as a bowl rest. With the other hand, I search *Raegan* and *Raquel*, along with *Picnic missing persons*. I try the names with *kidnapping* and *disappearance*. Nothing. I wish I'd asked the crossing guard if she remembered more details. The age of the girl. Or how many people were in her family. Anything.

It's also possible the woman was wrong and the disappearance happened longer ago—before the media put everything online. Or maybe it's all a story she once heard, which would be believable in the rumor mill that is Picnic.

But then I remember the play. The way the mother, Catherine, wailed *Where is my baby?* when she realized her daughter was missing. What were those first moments like when my aunt found the crib empty? Did she search the house frantically? Did she scream? Or crumple on the carpet in tears?

My own tears return, and Giblet overturns the empty bowl to lick my chin. The garage door startles me with its mechanical roar, and I feel a little wave of relief. I wipe my cheeks. Mom is still dressed in the sweats she pulled over her pajamas the night before. The skin under her eyes is lined and greenish blue, and her long hair, uncharacteristically, is pulled into a ponytail. I offer her the leftover noodles, but she wrinkles her nose at the congealed orange sauce in the pot and drops onto the cushion beside me with a groan. I lean against her shoulder.

"Anything?" I ask, afraid to sound hopeful.

She shakes her head wearily, and I glance at the clock. Almost twenty-four hours since Madison went missing. The crime shows my mom watches always talk about how missing children are rarely found alive after the first seventy-two. My throat tightens.

"How's Cindy?" I ask, my voice high and a little shaky.

"She needed to rest. She was with police all day."

"Do they—do they think it was her, Mom?"

My mom doesn't meet my eyes. She stares out the window to the forest. The mac and cheese curdles in my stomach.

"I don't know," she says finally. "I advised her to get a lawyer." My mom could have easily protected me, told me things would be fine, that Madison would come back and Cindy would be exonerated. But the fact that she admitted her own doubts? That means she's trying to prepare me for the worst.

I swallow. "Did they talk to Roald?" I ask.

"Yeah. He was at the riverboat all night. Gambling on camera, clear as can be." Disappointment leaches under my skin. It isn't that I *wanted* Madison's dad to be a suspect—only that I hoped Cindy wouldn't be the first in mind.

"Do the police have any clues? Anything to go on?"

She shakes her head, and I catch a tear glimmering in the corner of her eye. She sniffs, wipes it away with her sleeve, and nudges my foot with her toe—obviously trying to change the subject. "Did you do your homework?"

"Didn't have any," I say, which is sort of true.

"All right. I'm going upstairs," she says. "I don't have it in me to watch the news tonight. Take care of Giblet and make sure you don't get to bed too late, okay?" She stands, kisses her palm, and plants it on my forehead.

"Night," I say.

Once I hear her feet on the staircase, I turn my attention to the woods. A tiny sliver of the moon is out, and the branches seem to reach for it, fluttering and grabbing with each gust of wind. I lower my gaze to the black spaces between the trunks, searching for the gold eyes. They aren't there.

Somehow their absence is more terrifying than their presence was, glinting in the moonlight, watching me.

WE WERE WARRIORS

WE WERE WARRIORS *on the old-world battlefields. Slicing the sky with our wings. Catching men's swords in our teeth. Slithering into their camps and striking with our venom while they slept. Though we enjoyed battle, we did not choose it. It was usually the women who approached us to ask our help. They were not afraid like the men who ran from our songs. They thought of us as the powerful guardians we were. Behind the men's backs, they brought us cloth spun from their only wool, embroidered with vines and leaves— beautiful things we could not coax our own fingers to make. We loved to line our dens with it and curl beneath its weight. Protect my one true love, they'd say. We accepted their gifts but always asked for one more to keep our pack strong: a promise.*

10

FANYA

I SNIFF THE air. The woods still smell strongly of People Only. I heard their voices during yellow light, shouting a word I didn't understand. *Mah-de-son. Mah-de-son.*

Old One Zora lands above me and screeches. It's time.

I swish my tail at her call and slide into our Den. It is warm, dark, and damp like before a rainstorm. The Gray Forms scrape our dirt floor with their claws to find long-saved bones. I join in, kicking dirt. Air Forms pluck feathers. Earth Forms shiver and shake out of their skin. Teodora stands in the middle in People Form, her white head-fur tied back with ivy and leaves springing out from behind her flat ears.

The small fox-furred People Only watches from behind her stick cage.

"What doing? Where Mama? Where?" the Small says.

I tear a mouthful of my own fur and carry it to Teodora. She takes the dug-up bones and fits one to the next. Her tongue, pink and fat, hangs out like she forgets she is People. She wraps Earth Form skin over bones and pinches it with clumsy People fingers. She threads feathers in and out to hold it in place. She takes my fur and sticks it to the top. Last, she pricks the Small with a broken Earth Form fang. The Small screeches. Teodora carries the blood drop to the New Form.

The Pack circle-paces—*fwupp*ing and padding and *sssssss*ing.

Teodora places a hand on the New Form and speaks words I have not heard before. Old words.

The skin-wrapped bones begin to flush and bloat, the feathers absorbing into flesh. My gift fur turns from gray to red like it is lit on fire. The New Form wiggles, kicks, and sprouts digits from bone-knobs. The skin on its face dips into three hollows. I am *huh-huh-huh*ing in excitement and Teodora beckons me over the face of this New Form so my tongue-drips fall into the hollows. Two blue puddles form. It begins to look like the Small who gave it blood.

With one final word, Teodora plunges fingers into the third face hollow and tears the skin into a round hole. The Pack stops circle-pacing.

The New Form sputters, writhes. The face hole opens wide. *Waaaaaahhhhhhhh*, it wails. Just like the Small.

The urge to join comes from deep. I throw my head back and sing our oldest song. The other Gray Forms join. Our voices lift to the moon we can't see.

"Hurry, Fanya," Teodora says when our song is finished. "You must go before light."

I grab the New Form by its head-fur. It is heavy, but I am strong in haunch, foot, and jaw.

I run.

11

LUCE

Waning Crescent (1% visible), Friday, October 16

IT MUST BE about 3:00 a.m. when I hear my mom's cell phone ringing through the wall we share, because I wake and fall back asleep and wake again, trying to fight the inertia of unconsciousness. The pull is too strong, and I don't wake fully until my mom gently shakes my arm.

"Luce."

I'm still woozy with sleep, so I keep my eyes closed.

"She's home."

Through my haze, I don't think to interrogate my mother about the who, what, where, and hows, like a reporter. I say, "Thank God," and slip back into a sleep that is, at least, dreamless.

My alarm beeps me awake a few hours later, and it takes me a moment of lying in bed before I remember my mom's early-morning visit. I fling open my bedroom door and smell coffee—rich and earthy—from the kitchen. I skip down the stairs.

The sliding door is open and my mom stands outside on the porch, blowing on her coffee, her hair wet from a shower. I throw my arms around her waist and hug her. I'm shaking and sobbing—all that pent-up worry about Madison and Cindy leaking out of my face. My mom rubs my arms with her free hand. "That was my reaction too," she says.

I release her waist and she turns to face me. "Where did they find her?" I ask.

"In her crib. She was there, sound asleep, like she'd never left."

"What? So someone brought her back?" I ask. I'm filled with relief, but this fact seems beyond strange. She's a child—not a lost wallet.

"I guess so." My mom purses her lips like she's confused by this too.

"Did Cindy call the police?" I ask.

"Oh yes. I think they're pretty . . . surprised." I take that to mean *suspicious*. "They were at her house all night. And she has to take Madison to a lot of doctors today." Mom's eyes well with tears. "But none of that matters. She's home!"

"She's home," I repeat, wiping my cheek with the back of my arm, and ignoring the tiny pinprick at the base of my skull, warning me that something is off.

Giblet finishes her business, kicks grass behind her, and

then races up to us, ready for breakfast. I scoop her into my arms—even though she tries to wriggle away and licks at my mouth. I laugh and press my face into her fur.

When Anders arrives, I've barely finished changing out of my pajamas and brushing my hair. I hand him a S'mores Pop-Tart, untoasted, and then pull him into a giant hug too. He squeezes me back. His long arms feel like they are folded around and around me, like I am knotted in. I want this kind of joy every day. Over and over and over.

"Luce!" Ashleigh practically squeals when I get off the bus. "I'm so glad she's okay!"

She wraps me in a hug, spinning me around. I can't help laughing as the mums whir by in bright pink and orange blots. "We should do something to celebrate tonight."

"My house," Anders says. "Dad mounted the old TV downstairs." Anders's basement is unfinished like mine, but he found a roll of carpeting on sale downtown and has been scrounging furniture from garage sales, all for what he's been calling our movie cave. He found a velvet love seat recently. If I can devise a way to sit on it with Anders, we'll have to lean against each other, from shoulder to thigh.

I grin and exhale. It feels like I've been holding my breath for days and finally, I can take a big gulp of air. Mom is right. There's no point in worrying about why Madison disappeared and reappeared—not when all that matters is that she's back and I get to spend the evening with Anders.

As we walk into school, we're stopped several times by kids I barely know. "So happy she's safe," they say. It's as though the whispers and stares of yesterday were part of that bad dream I had.

It isn't until I walk into English class that I feel that pinprick again at the base of my skull. A woman with permed pewter hair and a pink cardigan stands at Mr. Kriska's chalkboard, writing the name *Mrs. Perch* in looping cursive. There's a paper lunch bag sitting on the desk instead of Mr. Kriska's Styrofoam cup of coffee.

"Where is Mr. Kriska?" I ask.

She turns around with a warm smile that shows off what seems to be a set of false teeth. "I'm afraid I don't know, dear."

"Well, when will he be back?" I realize I sound rude, but I can't keep the edge out of my voice. Madison is home, the day was heralded by hugs and sunshine. The police couldn't still be questioning him . . .

The pinprick is leaching outward, sprawling across the back of my skull, like a crack in a windshield.

She shrugs apologetically. "I get a call from a service, and they really don't tell me much."

I spot *Picnic's Promise* on top of a stack of papers on Mr. Kriska's desk, the gold lettering of the front cover catching the light—almost like it has been left there to attract my attention.

"Can I help you with something else, dear?" she asks, tugging at an earlobe weighed down with a heavy hoop earring.

"No. Thank you."

I take my usual seat near the back as the room fills with my classmates, and slide my phone out of my pocket to text Anders and Ashleigh: **Mr. Kriska is still gone.**

What? Two days in a row? He never missed a rehearsal last year, Anders texts back.

Do you think it has something to do with Madison? Ashleigh texts.

I don't know, I type, though it seems possible. Sure, he could be sick, but what if the police have something on him?

The bell rings, and I pocket my phone—not sure if Mrs. Perch will be as strict as our regular teachers. She shuffles across the line of desks, handing out a stack of papers to be passed back.

"Mr. Kriska wants you to get started on a research project," Mrs. Perch tells us. "You are to research an aspect of Picnic's history and demonstrate your knowledge of both primary and secondary sources, as well as how to properly cite them."

"Anything in Picnic's history?" Lucas, a kid near the front, asks.

"Yes, the topic can be anything about the history of Picnic—an event, a piece of folklore, a group. Mr. Kriska wants you to start with a question—something you want to know the answer to—to help narrow your focus."

I stare at the assignment sheet, trying to read the instructions, but all I can think about is Mr. Kriska saying this kind of thing *happens* in Picnic, and the crossing guard telling us about Raegan or Raquel, who reappeared the next day.

There's a box on the assignment sheet where Mr. Kriska has typed: *What's my question about Picnic history?*

What happened when Raegan/Raquel went missing and reappeared? I write. If I know the answer to that, maybe I'll understand what happened to Madison, and I can shake away the feeling spider-crawling across my skull.

I glance at the play again, its spine visible from the top of the stack of papers. It's probably nothing more than a fictional version of Picnic lore, but on the off chance that it has answers? I have to get it.

Mrs. Perch gives us the rest of the period to brainstorm and plan our projects. I watch her move around the room, leaning over desks and whispering answers to questions. When she's in the corner of the room opposite me, I stand and walk casually to the front, where Mr. Kriska has several low shelves lined with books for us to borrow. Being sneaky has never been my strong suit, so I try to keep it simple. I pretend I'm looking for a specific book, trailing my finger over the spines, and pull the largest one I can find—a coffee-table book on the art of Diego Rivera. I'm not sure what I'll say if Mrs. Perch asks what this book has to do with Picnic history, but she's still with a student, pointing to something on the assignment sheet. I carry it confidently by Mr. Kriska's desk, scoop up *Picnic's Promise*, and hide it behind the coffee-table book, then press them both to my chest. My heart hammers so loud as I walk back to my desk that I think everyone will hear, but no one even looks in my direction. I slide both books in my backpack and flip over my assignment sheet. There, Mr. Kriska has asked us to create our research plan and list the steps we'll take to answer our question.

I write: *1) Find out the name of the girl who went missing*

Then add: *2) Find out what in the hell is going on with Mr. Kriska*

After school, I walk to the salon—a small, squat storefront on Main across from the donut shop and between two antique stores. When I open the door, an old pair of bells tinkles and the smell of cinnamon and fried dough is replaced by the sharp scents of bleach and hair product.

Mom is at the sink with one of her regulars, Mrs. Griswald, whose bold zebra-print dress is peeking out from underneath the black salon cape. Cindy's chair is, unsurprisingly, empty, and I can tell by the unswept hair and the pile of towels at the back that my mom is struggling to keep up with things without her.

"Hi," I say.

"Hi." My mom waves for me to take over. I roll my sleeves up and lean over Mrs. Griswald, massaging the shampoo into her scalp with the tips of my fingers like Mom taught me. She has me keep my nails super short for just this reason.

"How was school?" Mom asks.

"School was fine," I say. "I have to do a research project on Picnic history."

"Ah. Did you know history is my specialty?" Mrs. Griswald looks up at me through a pair of round purple-framed glasses. The blush streaked across her cheeks is a bright fuchsia that almost matches.

"I did not," I say, combing the older woman's short locks with my fingers to pull the warm water through and rinse the shampoo.

"Mrs. Griswald was my US history teacher," my mom says, returning to the chair to clean her brushes.

"Oh, so you must know Mr. Kriska too?" I pump some conditioner into my palm.

"Anton? Sure, I know him. Worked with him for decades. His wife, Samantha, died a few years back. Kindest lady. She was sick for years, you know. Lupus."

My mom clucks sympathetically.

"They didn't have any children," Mrs. Griswald continues. "Anton always said he had plenty at school."

"What did you think of him?" I ask, trying to sound casual.

"A good teacher, just like his mother."

"But, like, what did you think of him as a person?"

"So teachers aren't people?" she asks with a wink.

I smile. "You know what I mean."

She smiles back. "Oh, he's a little out there, but who isn't?" She laughs and closes her eyes for a moment while I rinse her hair. "He got that job on goodwill for his mother, I think, but Picnic has really given him the short stick, if you ask me."

"What do you mean? Because of the Vila story?" I ask.

She nods. "So he saw a weird thing in the woods when he was a kid. Doesn't make him a bad character."

I raise my eyebrows at that. "People think he's a bad character?"

"*Bad* is the wrong word." Mrs. Griswald waves her hand dismissively. "About twenty years ago, a baby girl went missing, and Mr. Kriska kept saying the Vila did it. He was practically shouting it in the streets. Good thing St. Anthony's was already closed. Then the girl came back and all was fine, though it almost cost him his job *and* Samantha."

Mr. Kriska thought the Vila took the little girl? Did he think the same thing had happened to Madison? Was that why he wanted me to read *Picnic's Promise* so badly? I can almost feel the script calling me from my bag.

"I was just thinking about that girl this morning," my mom says. "I couldn't remember exactly what happened."

"Do you remember her name?" I ask.

"Rachel Magruder," Mrs. Griswald says without hesitation. "Her folks were going through a divorce and she was staying with her grandparents at the time. Caused a big hullabaloo for about a day and then that was that."

My mom leans against her station, the deep V carved into her forehead. I can tell by the way she's chewing on her lip that she thinks this story is weirdly similar to Madison's too.

"There was another before that one too, but, for the life of me, I can't remember the details except that the girl was fine."

Another? No wonder Mr. Kriska said it *happens*.

I offer Mrs. Griswald an arm to lean on so we can walk back to Mom's chair. Mom takes over, sectioning hair with her fingers and trimming the ends. I pull the broom out of the corner and am about to sweep when the salon phone rings from the back where the washer, dryer, and kitchenette are.

"Luce, can you get that?" my mom asks, and then presses her tongue to her bottom lip as she lifts another section of hair.

I jog to the back and pick up the handset. "Sunlight Salon."

"Luce?" It's Cindy's voice, ragged like she's been crying.

"Cindy, are you okay? How's Madison?"

"Can you just get your mom, hon?"

I cover the receiver. "Mom!"

"Tell them I'll call back," my mom answers.

"No, Mom. It's Cindy."

"Excuse me," my mom murmurs to Mrs. Griswald, and trots to me, brushing her hands on the black apron she wears for dye jobs.

I hand her the phone but hover nearby, scooping the towels into the washing machine.

"Cindy," Mom says. ". . . What's wrong? . . . I'm sure she's fine. She's probably just tired . . . What did the doctors say? . . . You need a night to relax a little. Let go of all this stress. We could have a glass of wine after I finish up here. Luce can watch Madison."

I stop, laundry pod in my hand. I'm supposed to hang out with Anders and Ashleigh.

"No, we won't go anywhere, I promise," Mom says into the phone. "We'll sit on the porch and have a drink so you can forget your worries for a little while. Luce can stay inside. Madison will be perfectly safe and happy."

My dream of Anders's love seat pops like a soap bubble, and the residual disappointment is heavy. I shut the washer door like I'm moving through molasses.

I return to sweeping with a heavy sigh. Mom emerges from the kitchenette, hands on her hips.

"Okay, I'll take the bait. What's wrong?" she asks.

"Nothing," I say, knowing my tone doesn't convey it. I wish, for once, she'd ask me if I wanted to do something instead of making decisions for me like I'm four.

"Won't it be good to see your baby cousin after these awful past few days?" she asks.

I nod, feeling a pang of guilt. She's right. I should want to see Madison more than Anders. My cousin could have been killed, but miracle of miracles, she returned safely. And hugging her will feel wonderful, even if I have questions.

12

LUCE

WE SWING BY Golden Garden for takeout and a screw-top bottle of wine. When we ring the bell, Cindy pulls open the door and steps aside silently. Her red hair is greasy at the scalp and tangled at the ends. Her skin, which has always been pale, has a grayness to it. The creases under her eyes are thick, like someone pinched the skin and held it in place. I wrap my arms around her, and she bursts into tears, her shoulders heaving against me.

"It's okay," I say, awkwardly rubbing her back. I'm not sure what to do about an adult crying in my arms.

"Here, here, let's grab some glasses and go on the porch," my mom says, gently peeling her out of my embrace.

I look around for Madison. If she's not strapped into a car seat or the booster seat, she's usually climbing on top of the couch cushions—*mounins*, she calls them, which is hilarious because she's definitely never seen a mountain in Picnic.

81

"She's over there," Cindy says.

When I turn my head, I see Madison on the living room couch. It almost looks like she's being propped up by pillows, her favorite fire truck resting on her lap, as though someone else positioned her this way. Madison seems to be looking at something. A spot on the ceiling? I follow her gaze, squinting, but I can't find whatever has captured her attention in the swirls of plaster.

I raise my eyebrows at my mom in a silent question. She jerks her head toward Madison as if to say, *Go on*.

So I do.

"Hi, Maddy," I coo. "Go, we'll be okay," I say to Cindy with my most confident smile.

Once they are out on the front porch, I approach Madison with my arms open for a hug. "Hi there, pumpkin. I'm so glad to see you."

She turns toward me jerkily—like those animatronics they had at Chuck E. Cheese when I was little. Her head drops to one shoulder and she stares, her eyes blank. I take a slow breath. Now I get why Cindy was so upset when she called the salon. Madison is clearly not the same after whatever happened to her.

"Let's play," I say, my voice shaky. I take the fire truck from her lap and make the *er-roo-er-roo* sound. She stares at me but doesn't join in or laugh. It's almost as if she doesn't know who I am.

"Are you excited to dress up like a kitty cat for Halloween and get candy?" I ask. She blinks at me slowly, like one of those baby dolls whose eyes close when you tip it, the eyelids occasionally getting caught mid-wink.

"Okay . . . how about some dinner?"

Still no answer.

I scoop her off the couch—she feels the same, heavy and warm—and carry her into the kitchen. She's a bit stiff, but I manage to Velcro her bib and strap her into the booster seat. I scoop rice into the compartments of a plastic plate and cut lo mein noodles with a neon-pink child's fork.

"Yummm. Rice and noodles," I say, handing Madison the fork and pointing at the food. She follows my finger, that jerky animatronic head turn again. She drops the fork and squishes the rice grains between her fingers mechanically. I take a few exaggerated bites directly from the containers with my own fork, making *mmmm* sounds, but her head lolls back like she is too tired to hold it up. How can she be so robot stiff and ragdoll loose all at once?

I try the old airplane trick, loading food onto the fork and flying it in circles toward her mouth. Her lips are slack and she allows me to place the food inside, but, a moment later, she pushes it out with her tongue so it dribbles down her chin. She doesn't even make the scrunch-cheeked *yuck* expression she made as a baby when I fed her squash. The food just falls out, and she barely seems to notice.

"Oh, Maddy, what happened to you?" I whisper, swiping her lips with a napkin.

Outside, I hear Cindy's voice growing louder and louder and my mom responding in a quiet, calm tone.

"That's NOT my child," Cindy shouts. It makes the hair stand up along my neck, but I clap to get Madison's attention so she can't overhear her mom.

Her chin levers down until her eyes meet mine. I scoot my chair closer so I can study her. Her irises are the same blue, but they seem shallower somehow, like the color is simply a contact someone put in, and there is nothing whatsoever beneath. I change angles, raising my head and lowering it—but her eyes stay the same. Completely flat. I brush back her hair. It feels coarser than I remember. I gently lift her top lip. Are some of her teeth slightly pointier than before?

Outside, I hear my mom say, "You've been through a lot. And so has Madison. It makes perfect sense that she might seem a bit different. Let's just give it some time."

What Mom is saying sounds logical, but I can't stop hearing Cindy's words in my head.

"Madison," I whisper. "Is that you?"

She says nothing. Just stares back at me, one eyelid dropping into a half wink.

WE CLAIMED

WE CLAIMED THE baby girls who were promised to us while they slept—their cheeks hot with dreams, their fists curled with power they didn't yet know—and made copies to take their place. We preferred the last-born daughters—weedy and wild, unwanted and unlikely to be missed. Ignored by fathers who needed another soldier or farmhand. By the mothers who couldn't bear another squalling at their breast.

Sometimes, choosing the last and leaving a copy did not work, and the mothers grew angry or heartbroken. They often did not remember the promises they'd made in the shade of our sylvan home, when they were pink-faced with love, when they, poor and powerless, wanted and wanted enough to trade anything. Send our daughters home, they pled or threatened, coming to us with their humble cloth or meager weapons, afraid to send their men lest they fall victim to our song.

We showed them their daughters, prey-fed and newly strong. Who could deny they were better off with us?

13

LUCE

WHEN WE GET home, I take out Giblet, who charges into the grass and to the edge of the forest like something is up. I hold her leash firmly, and that's when I see them—

The eyes. They're back.

I shiver and walk toward them a little, keeping my gaze trained on the gold orbs punctuating the night. The eyes are alive and as bright as small burning suns. Closer up, I can tell that they're lemon-shaped, like a large dog's, and they seem to be glowing on their own, not just reflecting light—the opposite of the way Madison's eyes looked earlier. I shiver at the memory of the emptiness I saw in them but try to push it away. My cousin is home, and I have to expect, after whatever has happened to her, that she'll be a little different. Like my mom said.

But why have the eyes returned?

"What do you want?" I call, backing away from the forest

edge and dragging Giblet with me.

This time, the eyes don't disappear when I yell. They just stare. Maybe it's a trick.

My mom is already in her room when I get inside. We'll have to be up early tomorrow, just like every Saturday morning during wedding season, when we drive to the smattering of Picnic-sized small towns across western Illinois. My job is to carry the bags into packed, chlorine-smelling hotel rooms, to roll bridesmaids' hair into curlers, and to hand fistfuls of bobby pins and clips to my mom as she twists the bride's hair into an elaborate updo. Then we head to the next small town and the next. We return home at dusk, backs aching and smelling of hair spray.

Even though tomorrow will be a long day, I'm way too wired to sleep.

Upstairs, I lower the blinds in case whatever is out there can see up here too. Then I unzip my backpack and dump the contents onto my bed. Finally, I can read the rest of Mr. Kriska's play.

ACT ONE
Scene Three

The sun sets over a sparse cornfield with spindly drying stalks. THOMAS walks up the dirt road toward his house and barn. He looks haggard and disheveled, his shirt untucked and hair wild. CATHERINE, already in her sleeping clothes, sees him through the window. She runs from their home and hugs him.

CATHERINE

Tom! I'm so glad they released you.

THOMAS

(wryly) Thank your father for us.

CATHERINE

He's not wrong, Tom. The town will continue to suspect us. There was no evidence of intrusion. We were the only ones home, and you have your history—of the nightmares after the rebellion.

THOMAS

I don't care what they think. Only what you think. You know I didn't do anything to our daughter, don't you?

CATHERINE

I never doubted it for a second.

They hold each other a moment. A wail is heard from the barn.

CATHERINE

Martha? Martha? Is it her, Thomas? Is it her?

THOMAS runs to the barn and emerges holding a baby. He cradles her to his chest. CATHERINE falls to the ground and starts crying in happiness. THOMAS sinks onto the ground beside her, and they hold the child between them.

THOMAS

My sweet Martha. Oh, my sweet, sweet Martha.

CATHERINE

(searching the baby for signs of injury) Is she okay?

THOMAS

She's okay. Look at her crying like she's testing out her lungs.

CATHERINE

But what could have happened?

THOMAS

I don't know. Someone brought her back to us.

CATHERINE

But why and who? You were in jail for this. Someone must pay!

THOMAS

None of that matters now, Catherine. She's
home with us, where she belongs.

CATHERINE

(turns attention to baby) Hush now, Martha.

Baby continues to wail.

Are you hungry? Yes, you must be.

Holds baby to chest.

Why won't she eat?

THOMAS

Give it time, Catherine. She's probably scared
and tired.

CATHERINE

She won't stop crying. *(studies baby)* Are you
sure it's her?

THOMAS

What do you mean? Of course I'm sure.

CATHERINE

(*looks at baby more closely*) No. This is not our
Martha. I know it's not.

THOMAS

Stares at Martha, concerned.

We'll get the doctor in, Catherine. All will be
fine, I promise.

CATHERINE

(*muttering to herself*) Something is wrong—I
know it. Something is wrong with this baby.

That stops me cold. My fingers are numb and tingling.
Catherine thinks the baby isn't Martha. I can hear Cindy again:
That's NOT my child. Is this a normal reaction after a child returns
from a mysterious disappearance? Cindy is short on sleep, and
the experience was traumatic. But the eyes, the hair, the teeth—
they all seemed different—and there's just no way that's possible.

I flip the page hurriedly and keep reading.

ACT TWO
Scene One

Interior of CATHERINE and THOMAS's home. CATHERINE is in bed, but awake and staring at the cradle as though afraid of it. THOMAS and MAYOR WELLS sit at the small table in the main room, speaking in hushed tones.

THOMAS

Catherine won't leave her bed. If I try to place the child at her breast, she yells, *That's not my child!* I don't know what to do, sir.

MAYOR WELLS

She'll come round. Even the most judicious of women have fits now and then.

THOMAS

I'm not sure that's what this is. Martha is . . . changed. But she *is* ours. She has to be.

MAYOR WELLS

Of course she is. *(stops as though remembering something)* I must see the child.

THOMAS and MAYOR WELLS enter the bedroom.

THOMAS

Your father is here, Catherine. Can you say hello?

CATHERINE remains silent and staring at the cradle.

MAYOR WELLS

Come on now, Catherine. *(waits)* Rouse yourself.
You must get up and tend to your household.

A sound like a screeching rabbit is heard from the cradle. CATHERINE shudders and covers her face with a blanket. MAYOR WELLS moves toward the cradle and peeks inside. He stares for a long time.

THOMAS

Do you see? She is the same, but different.

MAYOR WELLS

(backing away from the cradle) I must go. Now.

He rushes from the room.

THOMAS

(following him) But what do I do?

MAYOR WELLS

All will be fine, Thomas. I'm sure of it.

MAYOR WELLS exits. THOMAS is left standing at the door.

ACT TWO

Scene Two

Picnic Woods, dense with trees and undergrowth. Birdcalls are heard in the distance. MAYOR WELLS hacks at plants with his machete and weaves around trees. He seems to be looking for something and is muttering to himself.

MAYOR WELLS

I remember a stream and a circle of big oaks.

Like a choir singing, Old Woman Robya said.

Then the path, worn by their paws.

He points at the forest floor and follows an unseen trail to a hole almost hidden by a large rock.

There! That's their den!

He stands at the entrance to the den and shouts inside.

Vila! Animal-women! Come forth!

Three women emerge from the den, one costumed as a wolf, one as a falcon, and one as a snake.

VILA 1

Jeremiah, you have returned.

VILA 2

You have aged poorly. You are old for your kind, no?

VILA 3

Have you come to stay with us this time? You will make an excellent tree.

MAYOR WELLS

No, I have come because my daughter is very sick. She never leaves her bed and has stopped caring for my granddaughter. The child—well— she doesn't seem like herself anymore either. Not after she disappeared.

The VILA wait, silent. MAYOR WELLS clears his throat.

During the rebellion, you protected my sons and son-in-law. I thought maybe—

VILA 1

(interrupts ecstatically) Oh yes! What beautiful boys!

VILA 2

(sadly) Beautiful boys hunting one another. So much beautiful blood spilled.

VILA 3

And beautiful girls hurt—so hurt. If only we could have made them part of our pack. We would have protected them.

VILA 2

They would be fierce like us.

MAYOR WELLS

Wait—what did you say? You could have made them part of your pack?

VILA 1

Under the Forefathers' full moon, we can give one girl our powers.

VILA 2

Give her our strength.

VILA 3

Give her flight. And prowl. And sneak.

MAYOR WELLS

But how could you do that? (*pauses*) Do you *take* the girl? From her home? From her mother?

VILA 1

(to VILA 2) Perhaps he has forgotten what he promised us?

VILA 2

Have you forgotten, Jeremiah? What we asked for in return for protecting your beautiful boys?

MAYOR WELLS

You said a favor, but—

VILA 2

We have already taken the favor, dear Jeremiah.

MAYOR WELLS

You have my Martha?

VILA 1

A sweet, simple child.

MAYOR WELLS

If you have Martha, who is the child home with my son-in-law?

VILA 2

(shrugs) A leftover.

VILA 3

A changeling.

MAYOR WELLS

Our Martha should be with her family! My daughter—her mother—is not well! She's Heartsick and broken. I demand you return our Martha!

VILA 2

Don't you want her to be strong?

VILA 3

Don't you want her to fly? To slip between the grasses? To run with her pack?

VILA 1

Don't you want her to stalk the green earth, free, for as long as she wishes?

MAYOR WELLS

I want her with her family. *(voice cracks)* With my daughter. Return her at once.

VILA 3

It's almost Forefathers' Eve and the moon

grows full. The ritual is nearly complete. Soon
we will be her family. Don't worry. We take
good care of one another.

MAYOR WELLS

No! She's mine. If you will not return her, then
I shall take her back. My sons and I shall come
armed.

VILA 3

We are not afraid of your clumsy, weak bodies.
You are only people. We Vila live forever!

More VILA emerge from the den. The VILA circle him, getting closer and closer.

Do you want your soul trapped in bark? To live
on as a tree?

*MAYOR WELLS pushes through the circle and flees. They laugh but do
not follow.*

I feel like my blood is echoing in my skull. *A changeling*, the
Vila said. It's just a story, I remind myself, though it's a bit different from what I grew up hearing. I remember stories about Vila
shape-shifting into animals and turning men into trees with
their songs—nothing about them fighting in wars and people

giving up children as payment for protection. I wonder if Mr. Kriska's grandfather made that part up for the play or if the tales changed over the years, as stories tend to.

I try to clear my head, but I can't ignore the lines about the Vila giving one girl their powers and becoming her family by the full moon on Forefathers' Eve. I search *Forefathers' Eve* on my phone and learn it refers to Dziady, a Slavic holiday similar to Halloween and celebrated on October 31. I pull up a moon-phase calendar next.

I rub my eyes and open another website's calendar. Then another.

But they all show the same thing: a full white circle on Halloween.

I drop my phone. If something similar is happening now, to Madison, then I have just over two weeks.

I look back at the play. It has to be nonsense, but I have to keep reading to know for sure.

ACT TWO
Scene Three

MAYOR WELLS's *parlor.* THOMAS, *holding* CHANGELING MARTHA, *and* CATHERINE *are seated beside each other on the love seat.*

THOMAS

Say hi to Mummy.

CATHERINE

I am not her mother.

THOMAS

Hush, Catherine, not in front of the girl.

CATHERINE

(*listlessly*) Is it a girl?

THOMAS

(*to MARTHA*) Mummy doesn't mean it.

(*to CATHERINE*) Please, Catherine, I want her to know her mother. Come home, if only for a night.

MAYOR WELLS enters.

MAYOR WELLS

You know she is not well, Thomas. It is best she stays here. There will be less talk around town about the asylum.

CATHERINE

Makes wailing sound.

MAYOR WELLS

I won't let them take you to St. Anthony's, darling.

THOMAS

How is this better for her? You keep her locked
up here. Is she even allowed walks?

MAYOR WELLS

She is too sick for walks. You've heard her: *My
child is still missing. Where is my real baby?*
People think she's hysterical.

THOMAS

Martha needs her mother.

MAYOR WELLS

Looks at Martha.

I don't think she needs much of anything.

THOMAS

(*indignantly*) She is your grandchild.

CATHERINE

(*yelling*) She is not a child! She is not a child! She
is not a child!

MAYOR WELLS

Takes CATHERINE's hand.

Shhhh now, beloved.

Delilah! Please come take Catherine and put
her to bed.

*DELILAH, the maid, enters. CATHERINE wails louder, and THOMAS
stands to plead with MAYOR WELLS.*

THOMAS

You're killing her, Jeremiah. Don't you see?

MAYOR WELLS

No, Thomas. I am keeping her safe.

THOMAS stalks out.

ACT TWO
Scene Four

*MAYOR WELLS and THOMAS stand together in dark suits, hats in hands, in
a cemetery some distance from a fresh mound of dirt. St. Anthony's is visible
on a hill in the background. Three young men, CATHERINE's brothers, and a
few other TOWNSPEOPLE are clustered around the mound. DELILAH holds
CHANGELING MARTHA, now around six years old, in her arms.*

MAYOR WELLS

She died because of that awful place. I never should have let them take her.

THOMAS

They took her because she was hurting herself. She missed her family.

MAYOR WELLS

That child (*gestures at MARTHA*) is not her family.

THOMAS

You're as bad as she was.

MAYOR WELLS

Catherine was right, and it is all that old hag's fault.

THOMAS

What do you mean? What old hag?

MAYOR WELLS

The witch, Robya. Before the rebellion, she told me where to find (*with vitriol*) them. She told me to make a deal and they could help keep my sons safe on the battlefield. Even you.

THOMAS

Me?

MAYOR WELLS

I didn't want my only daughter to be a widow.

Laughs wryly.

Little good it did.

THOMAS

What deal did you make, Jeremiah?

MAYOR WELLS

I thought they'd want money, but . . .

THOMAS

But what?

MAYOR WELLS remains silent.

But what, Jeremiah? Did you trade my daughter's life? Your own granddaughter?

MAYOR WELLS

I didn't understand the terms. Don't worry. I will

make the witch pay. I will make them all pay.

MAYOR WELLS exits, leaving THOMAS alone at the graveside.

My eyes sting, and I blink quickly. Catherine is a fictional character, but I can't help thinking of Cindy. What if she tells people Madison isn't Madison? What will happen to her? St. Anthony's closed long ago, but Picnic has still shown itself unforgiving when someone stands out. Just look at Mr. Kriska.

I flip the page.

ACT Two

Scene Five

MAYOR WELLS arrives at a small cottage with mums growing in wooden baskets. An old woman, ROBYA, is outside, washing clothes in a large basin. She stands when she sees him. He rushes up to her, wrapping his hands around her throat. She tries to pry his hands off and sinks to the ground, so she is on her knees before him.

MAYOR WELLS

You brought them to Picnic. You told me
they'd help me during the rebellion. And now
I have lost everything.

ROBYA

Makes hacking sound.

MAYOR WELLS

You are a servant to demons, you old hag. You
witch!

ROBYA

(quietly, in a Slavic accent) Please—

MAYOR WELLS

They think they can take from others at will!
My granddaughter and now my—

Makes sobbing sound but shakes head to stop it.

ROBYA

(still choking) Please—I can help.

MAYOR WELLS

How can you help? My daughter is dead.

ROBYA

But your granddaughter isn't. Your real granddaughter.

MAYOR WELLS releases her. ROBYA hacks again.

MAYOR WELLS

Speak before I lose my patience. Start from the
beginning.

ROBYA

Rubs her throat.

They were being run out of the old country. I took
them across the ocean so they would survive.

MAYOR WELLS

Perks up.

How were they being run out? They have
powers and live forever.

ROBYA

All beings have a weakness. Theirs is silver. If
you chain them like goats, you can keep them.
They'll be nothing more than pets.

MAYOR WELLS

They will be mortal?

ROBYA

Nods sadly.

Mortal as you or I—as long as they are kept chained.

I hold the page, my hand shaking. Assuming these Vila exist—which is a big assumption—there's a way to capture them, which would mean there's a way to get back the children they stole. *If you can do so before the full moon on Halloween* . . .

No.

I shake my head. It's ridiculous. None of this is real. My brain is just searching for something to latch on to because this makes zero sense.

But I can't forget what Mr. Kriska said—that this *happens.* If that's true, Rachel Magruder has to be connected in some way. What did she act like when she returned? Did something happen to her mother too?

I pull my assignment sheet from Mr. Kriska's research project out of my backpack and cross off the first item.

~~1) Find out the name of the girl who went missing~~

2) Find out what in the hell is going on with Mr. Kriska

I add to the list:

3) Find Rachel and her family

I hesitate before I add number four. It still seems too unbelievable, but I have to tug at all the threads about missing children in Picnic, and so far, this play is all I have.

4) Learn more about the Vila

I pick the script back up.

ACT THREE

Scene One

Picnic town square, a grassy space lined with the MAYOR's grocery, a bakery, a bank, and the jail. MAYOR WELLS stands on a crate in the center with CHANGELING MARTHA, a large group of angry townspeople around him, armed with rifles, axes, whips, hoes, and mallets. MAYOR WELLS holds up a handful of silver chains. ROBYA stands a few feet away, watching, terrified.

MAYOR WELLS

I wrote to the silversmith in Springfield, and he sent every last one of his chains. The young among us have the opportunity to serve their town like their fathers and older brothers fought in the great rebellion.

TOWNSPEOPLE

Yes!

MAYOR WELLS

Hands chains to his sons to begin distributing.

I have shown you what these creatures are capable of. (*Lifts CHANGELING MARTHA's arm and shakes it until she snarls like a wild beast.*)

They have destroyed my family! Find them in the forest. If you see a wolf, falcon, or snake, throw this chain around its neck. Then what was once wild will be yours to keep or kill!

TOWNSPEOPLE

Hooray!

MAYOR WELLS

The promise I make here today is that no family in Picnic will ever lose their child like my Catherine lost our real Martha. For Picnic!

TOWNSPEOPLE

For Picnic!

TOWNSPEOPLE wave their weapons or shake their chains and run off stage left. THOMAS enters stage right.

THOMAS

Wait! Wait! Stop!

MAYOR WELLS

You are too late.

THOMAS

Jeremiah, what have you done?

MAYOR WELLS

What I should have done long ago! Protected
my town and its people from those beasts.

THOMAS

But if what you say is true (*looks at CHANGELING
MARTHA*), the real Martha is still there. Martha
is still there—with them. Our Martha! What if
she ends up hurt? Or killed?

MAYOR WELLS

She is already lost to us.

*MAYOR WELLS exits. THOMAS and ROBYA remain with CHANGE-
LING MARTHA.*

ROBYA

(*urgently*) Thomas, I will tell you where the Vila
are, but you must hurry!

THOMAS

Why would you help me?

ROBYA

Picnic has not been kind to me. They call me
a witch. And I've heard them call you just as
bad because of your nightmares.

THOMAS

Aye. They have.

ROBYA

Your Catherine did not deserve to meet her
end. And neither do these creatures, simply for
trying to survive in the new world. I shouldn't
have told Mayor Wells their weakness. Help
them. Help Martha.

ACT THREE

Scene Two

VILA den in the woods. THOMAS runs onstage and stops, out of breath.

THOMAS

Vila, Vila!

VILA 1, 2, and 3 emerge from the den.

VILA 2

One of our beautiful boys! Come to visit us!

113

THOMAS

(confused) Do I know you?

VILA 1

You are one of the boys we met during the
rebellion.

THOMAS

(shakes his head) I think you are mistaken.

VILA 1

Do you remember the day you were separated
from your regiment? You almost stumbled into
an enemy camp?

THOMAS

(dawning on him) One of the lookouts had spotted me and was pursuing me, and then a
wolf appeared and lunged at him, so I was
able to escape.

VILA 2

Claps happily.

Yes! He remembers!

THOMAS

That was you?

VILA 1

Who else would it be?

THOMAS

Then, thank you. I suppose it is even more fit-
ting that I warn you now.

VILA 3

What could you have to warn us of, fragile
creature?

THOMAS

The townspeople have silver chains. They
want to trap you. There isn't much time.
They're on their way to find you.

VILA 1

(*urgently to VILA 2 and 3*) Go see who is out hunting. Call them back if it is not too late. We must
abandon this Den and meet at the hill.

VILA 2 and 3 exit to den.

VILA 1

(suspiciously) Why did you come to warn us?

THOMAS

Because if what Jeremiah says is true, my Martha is with you, and I still want to protect her. To bring her home.

VILA 1

Humans are an inscrutable lot.

Makes barking call.

Another VILA emerges, with the child.

THOMAS

(falling to his knees) Martha!

MARTHA clings to the VILA.

(sobbing) Martha. Martha. *(reaching for her)* Don't you remember me?

MARTHA shakes her head.

Please let her come home with me in exchange

for the warning I have given.

VILA 1

It is too late. The ritual is done. She is one of us now and has begun to transform in her dreams. She needs to stay here, where we can teach her how to live as we do.

THOMAS

(standing) I can teach her. I will.

VILA 1

No, human. You cannot know what it is to slither and fly and race, to sing magic into the woods. We have taken good care of her and will continue to do so.

THOMAS

No, please. *(turning to the child again)* Martha, it's me, your father. I can take you home. Home, where your mama *(voice cracks)*— she used to rock you in the chair beside the cradle. You had a doll with yarn hair. I carved you that little pony. Remember our home, love?

MARTHA

This my home. *(louder)* This my home. This
my home!

THOMAS begins to sob again, head in hands. The VILA watch, unmoved.

THOMAS

(choking out the words) But will she be safe?

VILA 1

Our pack has survived a trapping in the old
world. We will survive again and build a new
den under great tree's ancient roots.

THOMAS

Can I at least visit her?

VILA 1

We will consider it, when the threat is gone, as
thanks for your warning.

ACT THREE

Scene Three

*MAYOR WELLS, now quite gray, stooped, and old, stands at a grave-
side. CHANGELING MARTHA, now a teen, is there too. There are a few*

TOWNSPEOPLE, *including the very aged ROBYA, CATHERINE's brothers and their families, DELILAH, and the PRIEST.*

PRIEST

Thomas was a devoted husband and father.

MAYOR WELLS

(under breath) If he was so devoted, my grand-daughter wouldn't have gone missing in the first place.

CHANGELING MARTHA *makes growling sound.*

(louder) If he was so devoted, he would have helped us catch those murderers.

SON 1

We caught many, Father.

MAYOR WELLS

(ranting) Many is not enough. We needed to catch them all. Their heads should be hanging on our walls!

SON 1

Let's go home, Father, so you can rest.

SON 1 and MAYOR WELLS exit. VILA 1, 2, and 3, and WOLF MARTHA enter and remain at a distance.

PRIEST

As we lay our brother to rest, we ask God to protect his soul and our own, so that we can one day be reunited. Amen.

TOWNSPEOPLE and PRIEST follow. ROBYA lays a flower on the grave.

VILA 1

In salute.

Throws head back and howls. VILA 2 and 3, and WOLF MARTHA join. Other howls are heard in the distance.

Lights fade.

It's quiet outside, but if I hold my breath, I think I can hear howls, like an echo from two nights before. I push back my covers and climb out of bed to raise a few slats of the blinds in my bedroom. The woods are dark—no eyes stare back at me—and the wind moves through the trees in gentle waves. If I press my ear to the window, the leaves sound like rushing water.

I've seen the ocean at night just a few times, when we were on vacation in Florida. I marveled at how utterly dark it was—

free of color and light. How you could hear the ocean even though you couldn't see a thing. The forest is that same impenetrable obsidian, undulating but never breaking.

I drop the blinds and pace, my mind whirring. If Mr. Kriska believed this story and tried to tell the police about it when Rachel went missing, then it's no wonder they questioned him. He could have called the police with the same story when Madison went missing. Or maybe they came to him on their own since he had come forward about Rachel. Two little girls missing is almost too much of a coincidence. And if what Mrs. Griswald says is true—that there was another one before Rachel—then this is a clear pattern.

I need to tell Anders.

I think of our hug this morning, his heart thudding in my ear, the heat of his chest on my cheek, the length of him folded around me. The memory of him, the comfort and closeness, it all makes me feel like I am shivering under my skin, deep in the muscles.

You awake? I text him.

I wait a few moments, but my screen remains dark. I flip off the lights and drop back into bed.

14

LUCE

New Moon (0% visible), Saturday, October 17

ANDERS DOESN'T TEXT me back until midmorning, when
I'm in a hotel suite with six chattering women in matching button-
downs and sweatpants that say *bridesmaid* on the butt. They're all
in curlers already, so I hover next to my mom, tools at the ready, as
she speeds her way through the bridesmaid seated on the barstool
in front of her. A makeup artist she partners with, Bev, is applying
eyeliner to another who can't seem to stop blinking.

Sorry! I passed out right after Ashleigh left, he writes.

No worries! I text back. But I can't stop the annoying
thoughts from entering my head: Did he and Ashleigh sit
next to each other on the love seat? Or did one of them
take the beanbag . . . What did they watch? Is he going to

122

invite her to our annual Halloween scary movie night too? I shake the thoughts away. I need to focus on Madison and figuring out what's going on in the next fourteen days. Once I get more answers, I'll tell Anders in person.

I give my mom a handful of bobby pins that she lines up in her teeth, and type *Rachel Magruder* into the search bar on my phone. There's a short news stub dated October 15, 2001, which seems to be just around the time the *Picnic Gazette* started to post their content online, favoring tiny paragraphs over entire newspaper articles. I take a screenshot.

LOCAL GIRL GOES MISSING

Two-year-old Rachel Magruder, daughter of Chet and Linda Magruder, was reported missing from her grand-parents' farm in Picnic, Illinois, yesterday evening.

The police investigation is ongoing and details have not been released.

There's nothing else.

Mrs. Griswald said her disappearance had the town buzzing for a day, so she must have come back quickly. But there's not another story when Rachel reappeared. The only reference I find is in a death announcement:

Trina Trappe, Picnic native, is survived by her husband, Marvin Trappe; her daughter, Linda Magruder,

née Trappe; and her granddaughter, Rachel Magruder.

But was it the real Rachel? Regardless, she must have an online life now like everyone else. Except I can't find a trace: no social media, no articles from a few years back about her playing on a high school sports team, no one with her name mentioned in a list of graduating Picnic seniors.

I look for an address for the Trappes, but I can't find that either.

Then I try searching more general terms, *missing children* and *Picnic*, to see if I can locate the other child Mrs. Griswald mentioned. News about Madison pops up, and I can't help clicking on the articles and staring at the photo of my cousin grinning at the camera with her stuffed duck, blue eyes practically twinkling. So unlike the girl I babysat last night.

I shiver and return to my search.

I find a social media post about St. Anthony's Wailer on an account called *GhostTaylor*. Taylor, who looks to be about Cindy's age, posts short videos of area lore—most of which are about the asylum ghosts. I pop in my headphones so I can listen.

Okay, so, the Wailer is probably our best-known ghost of St. Anthony's. No one has ever reported a sighting, but many of us have heard her, well, wailing. The story goes that, before the Wailer was committed, her daughter went missing. Even though her daughter was found not long afterward, the Wailer was sure that her child was still gone. Her family had her committed. She died twenty

years later and now wanders the halls, wailing for her lost child.

I feel a tingle down my spine. This version of the Wailer story is eerily similar to *Picnic's Promise*. Could Catherine be based on the Wailer?

I make a mental note to add to my assignment sheet:

5) *Find out who the Wailer was*

Once all the bridesmaids have cycled through, we pack up our bags for the next stop. As soon as we're in the hallway, I ask my mom what she knows about the Wailer.

"That ghost in St. Anthony's wailing for her missing child?"

"Yeah," I say. "Did you ever hear the part about how her daughter came back, but the mother claimed she was still missing?"

"No . . ." She draws the word out, and tilts her head at me. "What's this about, Luce?"

"Nothing," I say too quickly. I'm not ready to tell her what I'm working on yet—for school, or otherwise. "Did you ever go on a tour of St. Anthony's?"

She shudders and shakes her head, hitching one of the bags up on her shoulder. "I try to avoid scary things."

"Is that why you never go into the woods?"

"I've been in the woods."

I look at her skeptically. The light in the hallway yellows her skin and casts shadows from her brows onto her eyes.

"I have. I went to a Picnic summer camp as a child, and

the stories the older kids told made me never want to go back. I know it's all just made up and passed down to keep children from wandering off alone, but still—" She shudders again and marches through the sliding door as it whooshes open. It's cooler outside and we both take deep breaths.

"You let me go into the woods as a kid."

She drops her bags on the gravel in front of our trunk, patting her pockets for keys. "I didn't want you to worry about made-up stories and gossip. I wanted you to explore and just be yourself."

As we pull out of the parking lot and head to the next highway Holiday Inn, I can't stop thinking about what she said. When Mr. Kriska tried to be himself, the town said he had *one screw loose*. I don't want to be treated like Mr. Kriska, but something is going on here. Secrets have been buried, and I can't be afraid of discovering the truth. Not when my cousin's life might be at risk.

I text Ashleigh and Anders.

What are you doing for your research projects for Mr. Kriska's? I ask.

Something about the underground railroad house, Ashleigh responds.

Don't know yet, Anders answers.

How about a trip to the library tomorrow?

They both give me a thumbs-up.

15

FANYA

OLD ONES TEODORA, Nina, and Zora prepare for the ritual, gathering our lost talons and fangs in the shape of a moon on the Den floor. The ritual follows the moon as it changes Forms from shut eye to the Forefathers' open eye, the magic growing stronger each night.

Teodora waves to Nina, and she grabs the Small by her blue cloth scruff and carries her from the cage to the moon shape on the floor. As soon as she sets her down, the Small bolts, scrabbling with her little feet, but she is slow and clumsy like a baby bird. Nina picks her back up and plops her down. Again she tries, and again Nina catches her. I've seen mice do the same: run over and over as though you don't have them caught.

Finally, the Small gives up and sits, bawling, eyes squeezed shut, mouth a bottomless red pit of sound: "MAMMAAAA."

Teodora, in People Form, says her Old words loudly over the squalling Small. I can't repeat them because the Gray Form tongue is too loose. I heart-decide to be People. The smell of squirrel recedes and spoils until I no longer want to roll in it. Without my fur, my naked skin prickles and rises into bumps. My weak People eyes strain to see in the light coming from our tunnel. The Small looks like a fuzzy lump in the shadows.

When the ritual ends under the Forefathers' open-eye moon, she will have the power of deciding a Form. Someday, she will know her truest Form and live most of her life in that Form, like I am Gray. The Old Ones say she will soon forget she was born as People Only and live wild. Part of our Pack. I want to perk my ears and tail thump at the thought, but I am in People Form, so I flap my arms instead.

I try to focus on remembering the Old words, but something stops me. A thought pops into my head: If I am part of the Pack, and I can change Forms, does that mean *I* was born People Only too?

"Where Mama?" the Small whimpers. "Mama and Binky. Kitty cat."

I drop my arms.

Did I cry in a moon of teeth like the fox-furred Small?

Did Teodora and the other Old Ones chant over my Form? Did one of the younger in my Pack—Danica? Alina?—take me from a Den for People that smelled of charred cow and spring onions? Did she slip by while a light box was on and a Mother folded cloth? Did soft stars hang from strings above my baby cage? Did I sleep, cheek down, making tiny *snuff snuffs* before jaws closed on my scruff and carried me away?

Did I cry for Mama?

"Who was I?" I say the words out loud. Can't help it. Can't wait.

The chanting stops. Ten sets of eyes are on me. The entire Pack is staring.

"What do you mean, who were you?" Teodora asks. "You are Fanya."

My People tongue is slow and heavy. "Before I was Fanya, who was I?" I mean, *Where was my Den? Who was my Mother?*

"We don't have time for silly questions," Teodora says with a snort.

The ritual goes on. But I do not focus on the Old words anymore. I cannot stop hearing *Mama. Mama.*

THE GIRL

THE GIRL BABES were our seedlings, green and new, ripe for the powers we chanted into their marrow as the moon took its shapes. From closed eye to talon to tree knot to shell to round white unblinking eye, the new forms tethered to their bones, entwined with their muscles, pumped through the chambers of their hearts. Under the full moon on Forefathers' Eve, we carried them to the river and they became one of our pack forevermore, their first families long forgotten, their spirit powers exquisite in blossom.

16

LUCE

Waxing Crescent (5% visible), Sunday, October 18

MY MOM AGREES to drive Anders and me to the library and spends the whole time grilling him about his driver's license test next week. I haven't even been allowed to get my learner's permit yet. *Just because the state says it's time does not mean you're ready*, she says. In other words, Mom doesn't think *she's* ready.

"Don't worry, Miss Janice, I've been practicing," Anders says. "I promise I'll take driving Luce around off your hands."

"Well, we'll see about that," she says.

"We'll see?" This is news to me. After all that fantasizing about avoiding the bus, I just assumed that Anders's freedom would be mine too.

"Yes, we'll talk about it later," my mom says crisply.

I turn around and roll my eyes, and Anders gives me a wink

and dimpled smile. *Don't worry*, he mouths. My heart feels like it's doing a pirouette.

When we pull up, there are smiling paper pumpkins in the library windows—a reminder that the days are ticking by until Halloween and its full moon. *If* that means something.

Inside, Ashleigh has already set up camp at a table, her hair down and sleep-flattened. I can tell by the remnants of curls and glitter that she had a cheerleading competition yesterday. The library is relatively empty, with a few parents and kids in the children's section filling canvas bags with library books, and maybe one or two others in the main section.

Anders drops his backpack onto the table beside Ashleigh's and stretches, his long arms above his head so that his T-shirt lifts enough for us to see a trail of dark hair above his belt. I flush and look away, hoping he doesn't notice.

"Which way to local history?" I ask. Anything to redirect my attention.

"I think it's two or three rows back on the right," Ashleigh answers.

"What are you researching anyway?" Anders says. "I never asked."

I turn and clear my throat, not sure how my friends are going to take this. "I'm researching the disappearances of Rachel Magruder—the girl the crossing guard told us about—and perhaps other children, in Picnic."

Ashleigh blinks and looks like she's about to say something but then thinks better of it.

Anders's eyebrows dip toward the bridge of his nose. "Missing kids?"

I nod, trying to seem firm.

"But why?" Ashleigh asks.

"Because my cousin was gone and then came back and no one has a clue what happened to her. And this has happened before. Mr. Kriska was right." They look at each other, but I push on. "Wouldn't you want to know why if it was your family?"

"Yeah, of course, but you said it yourself—she's back now. So, what exactly are you hoping to find? And are you sure it's safe? Or, like, healthy?"

"Yeah," says Ashleigh. "Maybe it's best left to the police."

Are they right? Is this a bad idea? I think again about how Mr. Kriska claimed to have seen a Vila—one of Picnic's very own monsters used to keep children out of the forest—and then was shunned by the town.

"Would you prefer I pretend everything is normal? That nothing happened?" I ask. My voice comes out louder than I expected, and an old woman at the computer in the corner turns in her seat. A kid by the comic book rack stares.

"No," says Anders. "It's just that—"

"Well, good, because I can't. Something big and terrifying happened, and I'm not just going to be like, 'Oh well, she's back.'"

133

Anders shifts in his chair and glances at Ashleigh again. Something passes between them—I have no idea what—but it makes me feel like that third wheel, veering off course. "If this is what you need," Anders says gently, "go for it. We'll have your back."

It's a nice sentiment, but I don't feel particularly reassured.

I turn away and head to the stacks.

After about five minutes I realize that the Picnic history books are mostly about the Civil War and the railroad being built. The librarian, a short man with a red bow tie and suspenders, directs me to a section that has some Illinois folklore. St. Anthony's features prominently in one book, and the Wailer even gets a mention, but only to say that she wails for her lost child.

I ask the librarian if he has any old phone books. "You're in luck," he says, leading me to a reference section. "You are probably the youngest patron I've ever had request one of these."

He points to a set of thick books with yellow pages and much thinner ones with white. "If you're looking for businesses, you'll want the yellow. And people will be in the white. Remember that not many people use landlines anymore, so I doubt many of the phone numbers still work."

"But the addresses might?"

"Sure, if they haven't moved since the early aughts."

I take the most recent phone book off the shelf and flip to the Ms. My mom once told me that not every person wanted to be listed because telemarketers could easily find you, but it was also how she always found her classmates' numbers and addresses when she was growing up.

There are only a few Magruders in the book, but no Lindas or Chets. I flip to the Ts and, sure enough, I find a Trina and Marvin Trappe, with an address in the country outside town. I take a photo with my phone.

I settle into a computer seat and search *Vila*. I find several articles that trace the myth of Vila to South Slavic folklore. There are many variations, but in most tales, they are described as fairies or nymphs—often appearing as animals—just like in Picnic's story. And like Picnic's Vila, these also sing in a circle, turning men who venture near into trees. One article offers up something that stops me cold: the Vila steal children and replace them with changelings.

My fingers feel numb. I remember Cindy's voice, loud and strangled with pain: *That's NOT my child*. Catherine from the play: *This is not our Martha. I know it's not*. And the Wailer's gut-wrenching cry.

I ball my hands into fists and dig my fingernails into my palms until the feeling returns. Vila aren't real. Changelings aren't real. The similarities between Catherine and the Wailer and Cindy are just a coincidence. They have to be.

I pull out my phone and open *GhostTaylor*'s video. She seems to know a lot about the Wailer. Maybe she could help?

Hi! I message. **I'm doing a research project about missing children in Picnic. I saw your video about the Wailer and was**

wondering if you happen to know her real name. Or the circumstances of her child's disappearance? Thanks!

I return to the table, blood whooshing in my ears. Anders is flipping listlessly through a book about World War II. Ashleigh has a whole stack of books about the Civil War and the Underground Railroad in Illinois and is writing furiously in her notebook.

"Get anywhere?" Ashleigh asks. The question is innocent, but her lips are pinched with what looks like worry. I pause, wondering if I should tell them about babysitting Madison, the play, and all this stuff about changelings, but I know how it will sound—especially after they were worried about my *health*. I'll keep it to myself until I have something concrete.

"No," I say. Anders looks up, his dark eyes intensely focused on me. I try to make my face blank so he doesn't suspect anything.

Luckily, I'm saved by my phone buzzing.

Can Anders find his own way home? Mom asks. **We need to drop by Cindy's.**

Everything ok? I text.

Hope so. Be there in 2.

Now, that's a cryptic answer. I ask Ashleigh if she thinks her mom can drive Anders home. She nods.

"What's wrong?" Anders asks.

136

"My mom just needs to go somewhere when she picks me up. Sorry." I keep my face impassive.

His brows pinch together slightly. Concern, I think, but maybe disappointment too?

My mom doesn't explain much more in the car, only that Cindy called. When we arrive at her house, Mom walks quickly up to the front door without even waiting for me to get out of the car. I unbuckle and hurry after her. She uses the spare key to let herself in rather than ringing the doorbell.

When we get inside, I see why. The living room curtains have been pulled down, one end of the rod still attached to the wall and the other end on the floor. The couch cushions and pillows have been flung across the room. And there are shards of something blue and ceramic—a plate? a lamp?—on the carpet.

"What happened?"

"I don't know," my mom says. "Cindy?" She starts upstairs, and I'm about to follow when I notice one of the tweed cushions moving. Madison's head emerges, her hair fuzzed with static. She blinks at me as though she has no idea who I am.

"Maddy, are you okay?" I rush to the corner and lift the cushion off her. She doesn't say anything. "Are you okay?" I ask again, nodding encouragingly.

She nods back, but I think she's just mimicking me.

I check for bumps and bruises and then brush her strangely

coarse hair down with my hand, smiling at her the whole time, hoping this too will elicit some copying. She reaches for one of her stuffies—a whale—but her hand opens and closes stiffly, like one of those claws you'd see at an arcade. I pick up the stuffie for Madison, and she shoves its fin into her mouth.

"Where's your mama?" I ask.

"Ma-ma-ma-ma-ma-ma-ma," she says, mouth full of whale. It's the first I've heard her speak since this all happened, but it just sounds like meaningless babble.

I scoop her up, press my cheek against hers, and then pull away. She smells of her normal baby shampoo, but there's something musty beneath it—like the Christmas decor boxes we store in our unfinished basement.

I carry her upstairs, following the sound of my mom's voice to Cindy's room. Cindy is in bed, the quilt pulled up so that all I can see is the top of her head. My mom is behind her, propped up on one elbow with her other arm snaked around Cindy's shape.

Cindy lifts her head at the sound of me approaching. Her face is even grayer than when I last saw her, with a greenish hue under the eyes. "No, get her out," she says, her voice rising in pitch so it's almost a scream.

Instinctively, I cover Madison's ears and back away from the doorway. "Out," she screeches, even though I'm already out of the room.

My mom comes over, mouthing, *It's okay*, and closes the door gently between us.

I swallow hard, but I can feel the sting of tears. What is happening to my aunt?

Madison seems unconcerned and starts to chew on the fabric of my shirt—not just gum it but tear with her incisors. I pull my shirt away, and she sinks her teeth into the back of my hand instead.

"Ow!"

The skin doesn't break, but there's a small red half-moon. I have the urge to wash it with antibacterial soap like she's a wild animal. I put Madison down on the hallway floor. She crawls in a slow circle.

"Mom," I say to the shut door. "Mom, what's going on?"

My mom opens the door a crack. "I think we should stay here tonight. Tomorrow, I'm going to take Cindy to see someone while you're at school."

"What about her?" I ask, pointing at Madison.

"I'll take her to day care."

"No, I mean, don't you think she should see someone too?"

My mom looks at Madison, and I see a flicker of what looks like fear. "The doctor checked and said she was healthy and recovering well."

"She doesn't seem well."

"She did say we might see a little developmental regression. That means acting a bit younger than her age. Maybe not talking or walking."

Madison is still crawling in circles, her shoulder hitching

every few strides. It reminds me of a dog pacing in a cage. A rabid dog.

"Did Cindy tear apart the living room, or Madison?"

The V in my mom's forehead skin deepens. "I don't know," she says softly. "Can you call Anders to watch Giblet?"

I nod. My mom disappears inside Cindy's room again, and I sink down so I'm leaning against the wall, as far from Madison as I can be.

"What's up?" Anders asks when he answers.

"Can you watch Giblet overnight?"

"Of course. Is something going on?"

How can I even begin to explain this to him, especially after our conversation in the library? "Cindy's not feeling well." I leave out Madison, who pulls a piece of fuzz from the carpet and puts it in her mouth.

"I'm sorry," he says. "Is there anything else I can do?"

I take a deep breath, trying to keep it from shuddering. "No, I'll see you at school tomorrow."

"You'll see something else too," he says, his tone suggestive.

I rack my brain. What could he mean by that?

"It's my birthday . . ." he prompts.

"Oh! Your car!" I can't believe I forgot his birthday. I was going to bring him some Zebra Cakes, his favorite, and now—I look again at Madison and flinch as she begins to crawl-hitch my way.

"Mom is taking off to bring me to the DMV in the morning. I'm going to miss a few periods, but I should be there by lunch."

Madison scratches her fingernails down the drywall.

"Luce—"

"Yeah?"

"I'm sorry about earlier. I'm just worried about you."

"Okay. Thanks. I have to go." I hang up without waiting for him to say more. I bobble the phone as I try to pocket it, my hands cold and clumsy.

"Ma-ma-ma-ma-ma-ma-ma," Madison babbles. I stand up and back farther down the hallway.

17

FANYA

NINA SAYS IT'S my job to feed and water the Small before the ritual each night. Small didn't like the brown bird, so I try squirrel next, dropping a fat one with a thick tail at her blue feet.

"Mammaaa," she wails, her mouth drooping open so I can see all the way to the red bulb hanging in the back of her mouth.

I try crickets next—an Earth Form favorite. I let them hop across her hand, but she doesn't eat them—just makes a high-pitched sound like a rabbit and rubs her hands against her blue fuzz. I crunch them up with my beak, and drop them into her hand.

"Uh-uh," she says. "Uh-uh!"

What do People Only eat?

I fly to the side-by-side Dens for People Only and perch on a branch. The dark-furred Boy is in front of the glass, practicing his Peopling, but the Girl Den is dark. I swoop across the yard and a bright light flicks on. I freeze. Am I about to be trapped?

But nothing moves. No one yells or growls. I don't even smell the People Only or the fat rat dog. I change to Earth Form, feeling the ripple of soft scales and the binding of my limbs to my torso. I flick my tongue and slide across the remaining grass, hidden by its height. No one spots Earth Form.

I wrap myself around the handhold for People on the glass door, but it is too heavy to move. I slither to a hollow tube attached to the Den and climb it to reach a higher square of glass. There's some sort of metal material with tiny crisscrosses between my Form and the glass, but there's a small hole—just big enough for me to push through if I wriggle. The glass on the other side is open a crack, and I flatten myself into the space and slide through.

Inside, I smell something sweet and ripe. Orange fruits with thick skin sit in a basin on a flat slab of stone. I tap one and it rolls out and plops onto the floor. Nearby, I smell corn like in the fields near the forest, except the scent is coming from a stack of round discs in some sort of see-through material.

I heart-decide Gray—the only non-People Form that can easily carry the orange ball and the corn discs. I snatch the foods and leap back up toward the open glass where I came in. I shove the glass square up higher, but I can't fit into the hole in the metal crisscross material as Gray. I push against the metal and am surprised when it pops out into the grass below. I dart back to the trees, ignoring the light this time.

Back at the Den, I drop the orange ball and the round discs at the feet of Small.

"Orange," Small says, picking up the ball, her tiny white teeth visible.

Orange, I try to repeat, but with my loose Gray tongue it sounds like *Or-er*. She pulls at the skin, but doesn't seem to be able to get inside. The eye-water starts, streaking her pink cheeks.

"Maaaa-maaa!"

Wait, I try to tell her. I tear the skin with my teeth. It's bitter and I hack it onto our Den floor. But Small makes a sound like a bird chirp and puts the middle in her mouth. The bright juices drip down her chin.

"Dank you," she says, grabbing another handful of the orange flesh.

She pats my snout, and I lick her hand. The juice is sour, but sweet too. It makes my tongue buzz. I know I've tasted this before.

And then I can see it in my mind: a foggy memory of an orange without its skin cupped in small People hands. My hands! Is this from Before? When I was People Only? Did the orange bring this back?

There's someone else in the memory. A shadow moving across the Den as I bite into wedges of the sweet and sour fruit. She's making a sound with her mouth, really soft. A song?

Mama, I call to her, just like the Small, but when the shadow turns, there's a pale blur where her face should be. I can't see her. My Mother.

I paw my ears and let out a low howl.

THE CHANGES

THE CHANGES OF form always come in dreams first, fleeting and fast. It takes many new moons for the young to learn how to hold them on their own, how to choose a form and not be chosen. Then many more moons for them to learn how to fly and bite and slither and run. How to stalk and surprise and hunt. And finally, after their human forms go through their moon blood change: how to sing with their pack, how to perform the ritual themselves under the Forefathers' full moon.

18

LUCE

Waxing Crescent (11% visible), Monday, October 19

AT LUNCH, ASHLEIGH unloads the Zebra Cakes and birthday candles I asked her to buy on the way to school. I give her a few dollars, but I really wish the gifts had come from me. Anders is my best friend, turning his most important age, and I'm empty-handed, dressed in the same sweats and T-shirt I wore to the library the day before. I'm tired too, after sleeping on an air mattress on my aunt's living room floor, waking at every little creak. I don't even know how many hours I lay awake, looking at the sliver of the moon through the window, thinking of *Picnic's Promise*: *It's almost Forefathers' Eve and the moon grows full. The ritual is nearly complete. Soon we will be her family.*

I shake off the thoughts as they come back to me now, and try to focus on other things.

Anders walks into the commons wearing a cerulean-blue T-shirt that brings out the rich coffee-colored hues of his hair, and grinning like the world is nothing but Zebra Cakes. I paste a smile on my face and will myself to keep it there, even though my cheek muscles ache. He lifts his car keys in the air and shakes them. Ashleigh and I, along with some of his actor friends, cheer.

We aren't allowed to light candles in the lunchroom, so our table shout-sings "Happy Birthday" at the top of our lungs—even me. Anders blows out his imaginary flames, pretending that one of the candles is a trick flame that keeps relighting. Ashleigh claps delightedly when he finally gets it out.

"What did you wish for?" Ashleigh asks.

"Wouldn't you like to know," he says with a playful smirk. His eyes drift to mine and then quickly flit away. I don't know what it means, and don't have the energy to puzzle it out today.

I sit quietly on the bench while Anders flutters from one topic to another: how long the DMV lines were, what it felt like to drive to school alone, whether he is going to be in pep band this year or try out for the winter community play, why Mr. Kriska is still gone, and how he hates the smell of cereal milk. I feel my phone buzz and pull it out quickly in case it's my mom.

It's a reply from *GhostTaylor*.

Happy to meet another history buff! I work with the company that maintains St. Anthony's and we have all the intake records dating back to the 1860s. I was looking for

the Wailer and found the form for Emma Johnson, dated 1887. It described her as "wailing for her missing daughter" and "suffering delusions." The file also said her daughter had returned, but there was no other info. Hope this helps your research!

Based on the year, the Wailer is probably *not* Catherine. But this is yet another confirmed instance of a child going missing, then returning, and the mother swearing the child isn't hers. How many missing girls have there been in Picnic? And how many people know about this?

"Luce! Helloooo."

I look up. Anders is grinning, one cheek puckered into a dimple.

"Sorry—what?"

"You coming retro roller-skating this weekend for my birthday?"

I nod, trying to force a smile back onto my face, for Anders's sake.

After last period, I join the throngs of students crowding the hallways, frenzied with pent-up conversations and energy. Usually, I like feeling hidden by the sheer cacophony of it, but today, the reverberation makes my skull feel like it will explode.

My phone buzzes again. This time, it's my mom: **We're going by Cindy's to get her car and a few things so they can stay with us a little while.**

I swallow. That means Madison will be in my house.

Take the bus, she writes. **And don't forget to pick up Giblet from Anders's.**

Anders got his license today, I text back.

Which means he's still an inexperienced driver, Luce. We'll talk about it later. For now, bus.

I stare at the text, wishing there was a way to decline a message like a call: *No, thanks.*

Anders is leaning against my locker when I arrive, his keys already out and dangling from one knuckle.

"Ready for your first ride?" he asks.

"My mom said I can't ride with you yet."

"Is she home?"

I shake my head.

"Well, if she doesn't know, you can't get in trouble. We'll get home before her," Anders says. "I promise."

I hesitate. I don't defy my mom ever, but I can't imagine sitting on the bus without Anders's company and with all those voices—the middle school kids shouting about wrestling, the high school kids playing music loudly on their phones. I find myself nodding—not enthusiastically but robotically, as though this is the only choice my body has.

We walk to the back parking lot reserved for sophomores and Anders makes a big show of pressing the button so the car beeps. It's a silver sedan with temporary plates, bought from the pre-owned car dealership that used to be the train depot. We drop our bags in the back seat and climb in.

Even though it's used, the car smells new. I rub the gray seats and sniff my palms, wondering if the dealership uses some sort of chemical on the upholstery.

He checks his mirrors and flings an arm around the back of my seat so he can reverse out of the spot. He smells slightly of mint, and I feel the urge to lean in and sniff along the tendons of his neck and right under his chin.

"Look," Anders says proudly, hitting the button that opens a sunroof. The sun warms my right thigh in a small square.

"Is it everything you imagined?" I ask.

"In a minute, it will be." His eyes are on the brake lights ahead of us as we wait with the other high schoolers trying to get out of the parking lot.

"In a minute?"

He doesn't say more, but his dimple is visible as he taps his thumbs on the wheel. Once we get to the front of the line, he turns onto the highway that leads to our abandoned subdivision and picks up speed. He lowers the windows so the wind whips through the car. The sound washes over me, erasing the need to talk or think. A relief. I put my hand up through the sunroof and cup my palm so I can feel the resistance.

"This," he shouts over the wind. "This was what I wished for."

I glance in his direction. Does that mean I am part of the wish?

I smile and lean my head back. For a moment, I feel a little lighter.

We pull up Anders's driveway. Giblet is asleep on the couch when we let ourselves into his house, but she hops off at the sight of us and wags so hard she seems to be vibrating. I scoop her up and clip on the leash.

"I better get home," I say, still worried about my mom arriving before I do. I pause at the door. "Happy birthday, Anders."

"Thanks. It was a really good day."

He meets my eyes, and I can't help blushing.

Back home, I'm glad to find the garage empty. Anders was right; my mom will never know about the illicit ride, so I don't even have to lie. I put Giblet down in our foyer, and she skitters across the tile to the kitchen where her bowl is, as though it will have magically filled while she was gone. When she finds it empty, she looks at me with sad brown eyes.

"In a minute," I say. "Didn't they feed you over there?"

As I'm scooping the food into her bowl, I feel a cool gust of air. I freeze. Why would there be wind after the house has been locked up all day? I feel it again and track the sensation to our kitchen window. It's wide open, the screen gone.

"Hello?" My voice shakes.

I slide my phone out of my pocket and open the keypad to dial 911 if I need to. The living room looks just as it always does: The TV and speakers are mounted on the wall. My mom's

laptop is even sitting on the side table. I swing open the basement door and creep down the stairs. Giblet, now that she's
finished eating, hangs on my heels. Our plastic storage bins are
stacked against the brick walls, and the freezer whirs softly. I
poke the black plastic bag covering our Christmas wreath.

Nothing.

I check the upstairs next, sliding along walls and peeking
around corners. I'm aware of the quick clop of my heart, but I
feel focused too—like I could spot a flea in the carpet. When
I clear all the rooms, I return to the kitchen and look out the
open window. The screen is in the grass like something pushed
it out. I go into the backyard and retrieve it. There was a small
hole in the corner that my mom always swore she was going to
patch because flies would get in if we had the window open.
Looking at the screen up close, I can see the hole is wider now,
like something the size of a child's fist pushed its way through.

**Did you open the kitchen window when you were here
to get Giblet yesterday?** I text Anders when I get back inside.

**Yeah, just a crack because it was really stuffy inside . . .
Everything ok?**

I think so, I write, though I can feel my muscles quivering.
Something was in my house. I'm sure of it.

19

LUCE

I HEAR TWO cars pull into our driveway, and I creep into the foyer to peek. It's my mom's car followed by Cindy's. My fear breaks with a wash of cold sweat. They'll know what to do. They'll—I pause and look down at the screen in my hands. Cindy will get anxious and feel unsafe if I tell them about the window, especially after the break-in at her own place, and Mom will call the police, which will only add stress.

I trot back to the kitchen, shut and lock the window, and then stash the torn screen behind the door to the laundry room. I'll tell Mom later.

"Hiya, kiddo," Cindy says as she carries Madison through the door. She gives me a brief half hug that draws me close to Madison, and I smell her again. This time, the smell isn't just musty, but earthy too, like rotting wood. Madison's hair is pulled into her trademark pigtails, but one is lopsided, so it hangs like a limp dog ear. "Sorry about last night. I didn't mean to scare you," she says.

"It's okay," I say. "How'd it go today?"

My mom hauls the Pack 'n Play and a few duffel bags into the kitchen.

"Pretty well," she says, answering for Cindy. My aunt sets Madison down, and Giblet inches forward cautiously.

Madison pushes herself onto her knees and makes a growling sound at the back of her throat. Giblet backs away until she's safely between my mom's legs. I've never seen her afraid of a person before, especially not one she usually greets with wags and cheek kisses.

Cindy lifts Madison into the Pack 'n Play, and the toddler flops onto her back. We all pause, waiting for the usual screams. Madison hates naps, and especially hates being put in her Pack 'n Play for any reason, but she's surprisingly silent.

"Luce, will you keep an eye on Madison and make the tacos while I help Cindy get settled? The meat and fixings are in the fridge and the tortillas are on the counter."

They head upstairs, and I pull the meat out to start seasoning and browning it. I pick cilantro off the stems, quarter a lime, and shred a big pile of cheddar cheese for Madison.

The tortillas aren't actually on the counter, so I check the pantry. Then check the countertop again. I'm about to call my mom when I spot a trail on the granite counter. I sink down so I'm eye level with the shiny stone surface. There are tiny speckles leading toward the fruit bowl. I press my finger against them and lift it to my face. It's not kitchen dust or crumbs; it's dirt—black with hints of red clay. We don't have plants in the kitchen, and Giblet can't jump up to counter height, so how did this dirt get here? Someone broke in to steal tortillas?

Madison makes a hacking sound. She's been so quiet while I've been cooking, I thought she'd fallen asleep. I peek over the side of the Pack 'n Play, and Madison hacks again, like she has a hair ball.

"You okay?" I ask, but she doesn't even acknowledge that she heard me.

"Smells good."

I spin around, startled. It's Cindy, her hair wrapped up in a towel. Her skin is bright and scrubbed red-shiny instead of gray. Only her eyes—pink around the lids with dark puffed half-moons beneath—indicate that this has been anything but a normal day.

She perches on the stool beside me without even glancing in Madison's direction.

"How are you feeling?" I ask. I pull a head of lettuce out of the fridge, rinse it, and begin to chop it for taco salads. I'll tell my mom the tortillas were moldy.

"I've been better, but I'm okay." She takes a deep breath in, holds it, and exhales, just like she taught me.

I hear my mom's footsteps coming down the hallway above us. It's too much to explain what I've learned the past few days, but I want Cindy to know that I don't think she's losing it. I won't turn my back on her like Picnic has turned on others. Maybe it could have made a difference if someone had believed Catherine and Emma.

"Cindy, I don't think you're wrong." I glance at Madison. "Something weird is happening."

She sighs. "Luce, I shouldn't have said what I said. It's been a stressful few days."

I shake my head. "You don't have to apologize. I just want you to know that I'm trying to figure out what is going on."

She blinks rapidly and drops her head onto her palm, her shoulders rising and falling.

My mom pauses at the entrance to the kitchen. "Is everything okay?" Her tone is a warning for me.

Cindy nods, perhaps a bit too enthusiastically, and swipes at her cheeks with the backs of her hands. I busy myself with setting up the assembly line for the taco salads.

"And how's our littlest?" my mom coos, picking up Madison.

Madison lets her head drop back, but keeps her body flat as a board. My mom struggles to handle the strange starfish position, but she doesn't seem to want to lose face. She laughs, like this is a game they're playing together. Cindy watches them, her lips a tight line and her eyes wide with what looks like fear.

I know that look. And I feel it too.

While Cindy is putting Madison to bed, my mom sits next to me on the couch.

"Hey, honey. Homework?"

I groan, but I do have a US history quiz tomorrow—not that studying ever makes much of a difference. I find my backpack and pull out my notebook and a highlighter.

I chew on the cap a moment. "Mom, Cindy doesn't think Madison is her child. I heard her the other night." Mom narrows her eyes at me and gets up. She stands at the kitchen sink, wringing out a washcloth. "I wasn't eavesdropping, I promise. She was just loud."

"It was a traumatic experience," Mom says, wiping the counter in front of the fruit bowl and then lifting the rag and frowning at it. "The psychiatrist we spoke to today said that trauma can have all sorts of manifestations."

"But what if she's right and it's not Madison?" It's the first time I've allowed myself to admit the possibility out loud.

"Honey, you've seen her with her own eyes. Of course it's Madison."

"Have *you* seen her? Have you looked *into* her eyes?" I ask.

My mom leans against the counter, pressing her palms against it with what looks like frustration. "We've all been tired and stressed. The idea was probably planted in your brain when you overheard—"

"No. That's not it."

"All right, then. What is your explanation, Luce?" My mom's voice is thin and high, close to a snap.

"I don't know," I say. "But I wish you'd just admit there's

157

something going on here. Something about all this feels wrong."

We hear Cindy's feet on the stairs, and my mom presses her lips tightly closed. No way she's going to continue this conversation with her sister present.

"What's that?" Cindy asks when she's in the kitchen. She points out the back windows. I turn, pushing my notebook off my lap. The eyes are back, gold and still. I don't hesitate or try to talk myself out of it. I jog to the drawer beside the fridge and pull out the flashlight we keep for power outages.

"Luce," my mom says sharply, but I slide open the door and take off across the lawn to the woods.

"Was it you?" I shout.

I can't run very fast. There are too many divots and fallen branches that could take out my ankle. I nearly step on a rabbit carcass crawling with beetles and worms. I sidestep and hop, rotating the flashlight beam from the tangled shadows at my feet to the place where I saw the eyes.

I hear a flutter of feathers and then the whoosh of air being moved by large wings. I stop and aim the light toward the sound. I catch sight of a gold tail and try to follow it, but it disappears into the treetops.

I shine my light around at waist level, trying to find the gold eyes again, but they are long gone. I spot a small clearing up ahead, with a fallen log at the center. I walk to it, drop into a squat, and shine my light at the dirt around the log. Paw prints—larger than any dog's I've ever seen—circle the log, many times over. I jump over them, climb onto the log, and turn back so I'm facing my house. It's a fairly clear line of sight to our yard. The interior of our house is lit up, so I can see my mom and Cindy, both standing at the living room windows, their foreheads nearly against the glass. They look more like sisters this way than usual.

I'm certain this is where the animal with the yellow eyes sits to watch us.

I just don't know what it wants and why.

THE MEN

THE MEN IN *the old world began to multiply. They came for the bison first, slaughtering the great beasts with weapons that boomed. We hid in our trees and licked the blood from the dirt. They came for the trees next, wielding sharp blades on their shoulders. We sat on the stumps and watched as they built, log upon log, dwellings with clouds of smoke rising from narrow chimneys, great palaces marked with crosses, quarters filled with straw and beasts of burden.*

The more men who stumbled into our circle when we sang at night, the more who came in the light too, searching for our Dens, weapons on their hips. We laughed them off. They weren't a danger.

Yet.

20

LUCE

Waxing Crescent (29% visible), Wednesday, October 21

WITH CINDY AND Madison staying in our house, Mom and I still haven't had *the conversation* about Anders driving me to school. But sneaking a ride worked the first time, so I decide to try again this morning. I march into the kitchen, planning to make one breakfast instead of two so my mom will believe I'm going to ride the bus by myself. Madison is in her high chair, gnawing on one of our bowls, her teeth scraping against the ceramic.

Cindy sips her coffee, looking out the window above the sink as though she doesn't hear the awful sound.

"Here, use a spoon, Maddy," I say, pushing one into Madison's hand. She looks at it a moment and then bites down on that instead.

I can't get out of our house fast enough. I smear peanut

butter on untoasted bread, say my goodbyes, and hurry out, striding down the road until I'm blocked from view of my house by a stand of trees. Anders arrives a few minutes later, and I climb in.

Phew.

"The new Spanish teacher, Mr. Castillo, is taking over directing," he tells me as I split our breakfast.

Mr. Kriska is still absent, and Mrs. Perch seems to have settled in his place, her pink sweater now a semipermanent staple on the back of Mr. Kriska's chair.

"At least you'll have rehearsals again," I say.

"Yeah, but they'll be a joke. He'll never be able to pull off a play without Mr. Kriska."

"True, and you'll never make it to college if there's no play," I say with mock sincerity. Even though we're only sophomores, Anders has his parents record all his performances for potential college admissions materials.

"I won't!" He catches my smirk and knocks me with his elbow. "This is serious! I want to know what happened to him."

"I do too." *Find out what in the hell is going on with Mr. Kriska* is still on my list. "You said he lived on the other side of the forest. Do you know where?"

He shakes his head. "No. He just mentioned the forest before."

I nod, wondering if Mrs. Griswald, my mom's former history teacher, might have his address since they worked together for so long.

"Wanna come over for dinner Friday night? The parents are out, so I'm watching Jakob and we're gonna order pizza."

I grin, glad for the excuse to get out of my house and away from Madison. "Sure. Is Ashleigh coming?" I try to ask it casually, like I don't care one way or the other.

He stares through the windshield, one hand on the top of the wheel and the other resting on the bottom. "No. Football game," he says tonelessly, but I can tell by the tiny twitch in his temple that he's trying not to smile.

Mrs. Perch brings us to the library for first period so that we can work on our research projects. I consult my list.

~~1) Find out the name of the girl who went missing~~

2) Find out what in the hell is going on with Mr. Kriska

3) Find Rachel and her family

4) Learn more about the Vila

5) Find out who the Wailer was

I cross off number 5 and add—

6) Find out if there are any more missing girls

I sign on to one of the library computers, envisioning the paw prints around the log and the howls the night Madison went missing. Returning to the same spot night after night to watch humans doesn't seem to be very wolflike behavior. Could a wolf go through a screen to get into someone's house?

I find the website for the wolf sanctuary near our town. The animals on the home page are all thick-furred and healthy-looking, fuller-bodied than their wild counterparts I've seen in

National Geographic photos. Their eyes aren't so much yellow as a light brown and their coats range in color from white to black, with most falling somewhere in the middle—a gray with gold-brown undertones. Some are quite tall—taller than most dogs—though the majority look like they'd be waist height or shorter.

I stick my headphones in, click on an audio clip, and listen to the sanctuary's wolves howling. What I heard behind my house sounded exactly like these wolves.

I scroll down further and click on the link to FAQs. That's where I find what I'm looking for—

Question: Where do wild gray wolves live in the US?

Answer: Alaska, Idaho, Michigan, Minnesota, Montana, Wisconsin, Wyoming, and occasionally Washington, North Dakota, and South Dakota.

There are no wild wolves in Illinois.

Another question asks how wolves hunt—usually in pairs or small groups, I learn. There is nothing about wolves attacking humans or breaking into their houses, and certainly nothing about kidnapping children and replacing them with terrifying doppelgangers. Clearly, whatever I saw was not a normal wolf, if it was even a wolf at all. But what are the alternatives? Magical creatures that can appear as wolves and trap men by singing?

I loved fantasy books as a kid, delighting in creatures that were beyond belief: trees that talked, half-human-half-goats that played flutes, trolls that wandered the mountains. These fantasies shaped Anders's and my play for years. We could transport ourselves anywhere, be anything: leaders of a nomadic troop of witches, elven warriors, heroes. I enjoyed making up these stories, and always assumed they were just that. I never thought of them as real.

But what if they are?

"Wolves?" Mrs. Perch says, leaning down over my shoulder. Her perfume is cloying and floral, like the potpourri my gran keeps in her guest bathroom.

"It's nothing. Just a tangent," I say, crossing off *Learn more about the Vila* on my list.

"Tangents are part of the process," she says. Her false teeth make a sucking sound when she talks. "Is there anything I can help you with?"

"Maybe. Do you know where I would find missing children's reports from like the late 1800s until now?"

"Hmmm. Well, the police, but I doubt the reports go back that far. And you'll have to do what is called a Freedom of Information Act Request to get what they do have. It can take quite some time."

I frown.

"Another option would be to see if the local library has a

microfilm collection. That's how many libraries preserved old newspapers until we had the kind of scanners and digital archives we have today."

That seems exactly like something Picnic would do to preserve the past.

After school, I text my mom and ask if I can walk to the public library to work on my project instead of the salon. Since Cindy is back at work and Madison is in day care, I figure she won't miss me too much.

The librarian leads me to a small room behind the main desk where they keep the microfilm reader. It looks like an outdated computer with a set of buttons and knobs beneath. He shows me how to load the films, slide them under the lens, and advance using the large knob.

"Where do you want to start?" he asks, gesturing at the beige filing cabinets that line the walls.

I think about Catherine and the year listed in *Picnic's Promise*. "1868."

"There aren't many records saved from back then, but we do have a few." He pulls open a drawer, and takes out small narrow boxes labeled with barcodes.

The *Picnic Gazette* in 1868 is a weekly broadsheet, crammed with tiny text, each brief story demarcated by a flourish above a small bold headline. It takes me a while to get used to scanning the crowded text about cow sales and labor movements with the knob. I move slowly, until finally, I find something interesting dated October 13, 1868.

MISSING CHILD RETURNS

Constable Collins confirms that the grandchild of Mayor Wells (daughter of Thomas Greenley and Catherine Greenley, neé Wells) has returned safely to her home. No evidence of foul play has been discovered. Mr. Wells says the child is happy and well dispositioned.

There it is—proof that the play is based on a true story. I flip through the remaining newspapers for that year, looking for an article about Martha's behavior after she returned, and Catherine's decline, but there are no other references.

I try 1887 next, hoping to find something about Emma, but the few newspapers that have been preserved from that year don't mention anything about a missing child. I glance at my watch. I have another hour before my mom is finished at the salon.

I jot down the years on my assignment sheet and do the math. Nineteen years apart. Something is niggling at the back of my brain. I pick up my phone and type: *How often does the full moon fall on Halloween?*

Before I even read the answer, I have a feeling I know what it will be: *Roughly every nineteen years.*

My hair stands on end, but I don't waste time. *1887+19 =1906.* I find the box for October.

OCTOBER 16, 1906

LOCAL GIRL DISAPPEARS

Florence Ashby, 3, went missing yesterday. Mr. Ashby said she was last seen at the stream behind their house with their collie. The collie has not been located. Police are conducting searches of the nearby woods and invite readers to assist with the investigation.

My heart gallops. I add the year and name to my list and pull the box for October 1925.

October 15, 1925. Helen Banks. A two-year-old who reappeared a day later, with one eyewitness claiming he saw a large white dog with her.

October 17, 1944. Dorothy Richards. She was eighteen months old, taken from her stroller at a picnic.

My phone buzzes.

Be there in a few, Mom texts.

I slide the film back into their boxes and drop my pencil. A girl disappears every nineteen years, roughly two weeks before Halloween, and returns a day or two later. I have to tell the police. I have to warn other families. But . . . the crossing guard, Mrs. Griswald, even my mom remembered missing girls. If Picnic loves its scary stories, how come no one tells this one?

No, that's not right. Someone does: Mr. Kriska.

I don't want to bombard—or worse, alarm—my mom with this

168

as soon as she picks me up, so I wait until she's cooking and distracted.

"Mom, do you have Mrs. Griswald's phone number?" I ask while she stirs chili on the stove. "I need to ask her something for my project." Cindy is on the couch, warily watching Madison crawl after Giblet.

"Sure, hon." She hands me her phone so I can copy the number to my own. "What's your project about again?"

"We have to find primary and secondary sources on a topic in Picnic's history," I say, sidestepping the question.

"What did you pick?"

"The Underground Railroad," I lie, typing a quick text message to Mrs. Griswald. What I really need is Mr. Kriska's address. Before my mom can ask any follow-up questions, we're interrupted by Madison's screeches.

"Maddy, no!" She's crawling fast at Giblet, who tucks her tail and bolts for the laundry room.

Cindy reaches for her, but Madison bares her teeth and snaps. Cindy backs up. "Not again," she says.

"Again?" I repeat.

Madison lunges for the couch and sinks her teeth into the gray cushion. She pulls, managing to yank the cushion from the frame—impressive jaw strength for someone so small. She pivots for the floor lamp next, grabbing the pole as though she wants to strangle it. When strangling doesn't yield anything, she pulls until it tips. The bulb makes a tinkling sound—

169

smashed—inside the shade. She puts my mom's laptop cord in her mouth and bites down, shaking it the way Giblet does a toy. The whole time, she's emitting a deep humming sound in the back of her throat, like a hive of bees.

"Maddy, calm down," Cindy says, her voice quavering.

My mom drops the wooden spoon and pulls a blanket off the armchair. She throws it over Madison, wraps her arms around the bundle, and then lifts the struggling child into the Pack 'n Play. The bundle bucks, like a horse trying to throw off a rider. When Madison finally frees herself from the cover, she hisses at us, her hair a wild nest of static, her eyes empty and flat.

"We have to go," Cindy says, tears starting in the corners of her eyes. "We can't stay here or she'll destroy your house too."

"Nonsense," my mom says, but she's breathing heavily. "You're staying. It's fine."

I glance at the laundry room, where Giblet is peeking around the corner, shaking. I'm not so convinced.

21

FANYA

THE PEOPLE ONLY returned, so I couldn't get more of the oranges, and we're out of corn discs. Nina couldn't resist. I sniff the air and smell apples. I trot down the stream to a field of trees with pink and green fruit. Birds have pecked most of the ones on the ground, and the rest are too high for my Gray form. I turn People and carefully move my fingers to pluck one that is all pink. Even with my People nose, it smells ripe and sweet.

Oh, the earth is good to me,
And so I thank the earth,
For giving me the things I need:
The sun and the rain and the apple seed.
Oh, the earth is good to me.

The words spring into my head to a tune. Is it a song? What does it mean? And where did it come from? Danica? Alina?

171

No, I hear it in a voice, a People Only voice, warm and soft—like the one that sang softly while I ate the orange wedges. These words are from Before. From the foggy part of memory, where everything is blurs of colors and sounds. From . . . my Mother?

I try to find a People face in the fog to match the voice. What color fur? What color eyes? Does the face look like mine when I practice Peopling by the stream? But, just like before, I can't see her.

My eyes are runny with water, but I carry the apple back. I crawl to the stick cage where the Small sits, her blue fuzz now dark gray and caked with dirt, and place the apple in her hand. "Apple," I say.

Small looks at the apple, then up at me. "Help," she says.

I take a bite to break the skin for her and hand it back.

She takes a mouse nibble.

"Bigger," I say. I take another bite, this time sinking my flat people teeth in and shaking my head like I'm a Gray with prey. She makes a high, soft *he-he-he-he* sound and copies me.

"Yummy," she says.

I flap my arms because I can't swish my tail. I'll find more. I'll run for miles if I have to. Anything to hear this happy sound, to remember the song again, and maybe, just maybe, see the face who once sang it.

22

LUCE

Waxing Crescent (39% visible), Thursday, October 22

I TEXT MY mom that I need to go to the library again after school, and find Anders in the auditorium instead. The house-lights are up, emphasizing the worn red seat cushions, the aisle carpeting grayed with age and dirt, the runs in the heavy velvet curtain, and the scuffed caramel wood of the stage.

"You know I have rehearsal," he says, pulling a script out of his backpack.

"You said it was a joke," I point out.

"Yeah, but I'm still the lead. Can't it wait until this weekend?"

I picture Madison, tearing at the couch cushion with her teeth, the moon already more than a quarter full, according to the calendar on my phone. "No, it can't."

He must see the urgency in my face, though, because his eyes widen and his brows dip in concern.

"Madison is acting super strange, and Cindy is upset about it," I continue. "And I'm just hoping the family of the last girl to go missing can help."

"And what do you mean by 'strange'?"

I'm not sure where to begin, so I just say, "She's not herself."

"Well, she's been through a lot. It must have been a pretty terrifying experience."

"Yeah, which is why I have to figure out what happened before," I say. "With the last girl, Rachel."

He meets my eyes, and I feel a locking sensation—like he's holding me with his gaze. "Okay. We'll go."

We pass a soybean field and head up a long drive lined with tall browning grasses. A two-story farmhouse sits on a mowed hill with a large jack-o'-lantern on its porch. The windows are divided into six small panes, the glass wavy with age. The white paint is peeling, and the front porch appears to be bowing in the middle. The barn behind the house has long outlived its paint. It's missing a roof and several slats and looks like a wolf could blow it down. There's a newer barn beside it, a long, low building with metal garage doors.

We park on the gravel drive and approach cautiously in case we're facing a shotgun-wielding farmer, but there's no sign of anyone, just a vintage pickup truck with green paneling parked near the old barn.

We climb the stairs to the porch, avoiding the bowed area

in case it's about to collapse, and knock.

An older man answers the door. He is taller than Anders, straight-backed, long-faced, and bald with a white Santa's beard. One of his eyes is cloudy with a cataract. He wears the typical Picnic farmer's garb: jeans, a button-down cotton shirt printed with plaid, suspenders, and a large oval belt buckle.

"Mr. Trappe?" I ask hopefully. Farmers don't give up their family's land if they don't have to, so the phone book has a chance of being right—despite how old it is.

He closes his bad eye and glares at me out of the other. "Whatcha selling? I got enough candy."

I swallow. "Not selling anything. I'm Luce and this is my friend Anders. We're here about your granddaughter, Rachel."

He squints again. "Come in."

He leads us into a sitting room filled with furniture that appears well cared for—the wood polished, the velvet cushions free of dust. The carpet is spotless, with no sign of imprints from legs or feet or other wear. He invites us to sit on a pink settee, pulls out a pipe, and stands, leaning on the mantel. It's an elegant pose, like we are here to paint him.

"My cousin went missing and came back a day later," I say. "You may have heard on the news."

He waits, stuffing his pipe. No indication of whether he has heard me—or this news. There's a cry from somewhere upstairs in the house—a yowl like a cat's—but he ignores this too.

I clear my throat and continue: "I was told the same thing

happened to your granddaughter. It must have been horrible."

"It was the worst day of my life," he says, closing his bad eye again. The open eye reddens. He doesn't light the pipe, just pinches it in the corner of his mouth so he can only talk out of half.

"Madison, my cousin, has been acting different since she came back, and I was wondering if—"

"Like a possessed doll," he interrupts me.

"Excuse me?"

"She acting like a possessed doll?"

I blink, thrown by the frankness of this. Anders looks at me, one eyebrow raised. "Yeah, exactly," I say.

"Doctors said it was to be expected, but boy, they did not expect to be bit by a growling baby girl," he says. I hear the sound again above us; this time it's more human. A sob? Mr. Trappe's open eye finds the ceiling for a moment before returning to my face.

"Where is she now?" I ask.

"Rachel?"

I nod.

"With her father down south. It was better that way after the divorce. She comes up for the holidays."

"And is she . . . back to how she was before?" I ask.

"Before? No." He chuckles dryly like *before* is a funny memory. "I suppose she's less wild, but she went to a special school for quite some time. She barely talks. She can't do things like other young women: go to college, work a job, date. As far as I can tell, she just stares out the window all day."

He takes a framed photo off his mantel and hands it to me. "A few years ago," he says by way of explanation.

A teenager is seated beside a Christmas tree. She is long-faced and long-limbed like her grandfather, her hair thick and dark, springing from her head like she's an '80s rocker. Her eyes, though, are what stop me. They're a pale blue, and they appear flat—like buttons—just like Madison's. I swallow and swallow again, trying to find words so I can continue.

"Do the police know what happened?" Anders asks.

Mr. Trappe shakes his head. "They thought we should count our blessings and that's that. But you know the Picnic police are about as bright as shadows."

"So you never found out anything more about what happened?" I ask, my voice a croak.

"Some folks in town have theories." I wonder if he's talking about Mr. Kriska. "But ain't no theories that'll bring her back."

Above, I hear footsteps—pacing back and forth. "Is someone else home?" Anders asks.

"My daughter, Linda," Mr. Trappe says, looking at the ceiling again.

"Oh, I didn't know she was here," I say. "Can we speak to her?"

"Another time. She isn't having one of her . . . better days," he says.

I look at the ceiling again, wondering if this is Cindy's future.

Mr. Trappe walks us out, and I'm completely spent. But I have to get back to the library quickly so my mom can find me there when she's done at the salon. I don't want to lose the privilege of riding with Anders before I've even gained it.

"What are you thinking?" Anders asks, eyes flicking between me and the road.

I open my mouth and then shut it, shaking my head. I can't say it out loud yet. Rachel, the possessed doll. Rachel, who looks okay but isn't. Who barely talks and spends all day staring out the window, empty-eyed. It all spells changeling.

"I have to talk to Mr. Kriska. I got his address from my mom's client," I tell Anders. "Maybe we can go tomorrow while your parents are out?"

"I have to watch Jakob."

"Oh, right. Sunday before roller-skating?"

Anders nods.

I need to find out what Mr. Kriska knows and why he's gone.

When Mom and I get home, the Pack 'n Play isn't in the living room. All of Cindy's stuff is gone from the guest bedroom too. There's a Post-it on the mirror that says only: *Thank you* ❤

"She said she wanted to drive separately this morning." My mom sounds hurt. "I should have said no."

I make a sympathetic sound but feel a wave of relief that I don't have to see Madison—not after what I learned today.

178

Downstairs, I stick frozen lasagna in the oven while my mom calls Cindy. No answer. Mom arranges the place mats—all four as though Cindy might still show up. "I should go over there," she says.

"Maybe she needs a little space and time to find a new normal after all this," I say.

She looks up at me, surprised, I think. "I suppose you're right. That's a very mature perspective."

I swallow, recognizing my window, and try to gather my resolve. "Speaking of," I say cautiously, "I'd like to ride with Anders this weekend. He's going to help me with my research and then we're going roller-skating with some friends for his birthday." I leave out Mr. Kriska. She doesn't need to know everything.

"Luce, I'm not—"

"I know he just got his license. But he's been practicing with his dad and he's a really safe driver!"

She sighs and appears to be making up her mind. "Okay. Ground rules: you always tell me exactly where you're going, who you're going with, and text me when you get there. If you break any of those, then no more rides."

I can't help smiling.

THE OLD WORLD

THE OLD-WORLD QUEEN who led to the first trapping found us as many other women had, feverish with love. Her arms were laden with gifts of white cloth that glimmered with small pearls the likes of which we had never seen. Her hair shone like firelight and her eyes were the color of moss. There is an uprising, *she told us.* My love, the king, is in danger. *We thought nothing of her uprisings or kings. Only of that cloth—like snow on a winter's eve—and the future babe, a smoldering seed deep inside. We licked our teeth, polished our beaks, and barked* yes, *forgetting how the moon can be a snake eating its own tail.*

23

LUCE

First Quarter (50% visible), Friday, October 23

I SPEND WAY longer in the mirror than usual, trying to style my bob with my mom's hair paste so the asymmetrical part of it doesn't just hang limp to my chin. It ends up looking sticky, and I run water through it to wash it out. I stare at myself, one section of hair dripping down my cheek and the rest dry and coarse. My mom, Cindy, and I all share green eyes that, in sunlight, are the color of evergreens. My eyes were blue when I was born but shifted over time, and I wonder if Madison's will do the same.

I feel a punch of fear that I won't get to find out. Halloween is just over a week away, so if all this is true, I have just eight days to figure out what is going on and find the real Madison.

I pull on a pair of jeans and a long-sleeved blouse that drops off my shoulders. I dot a tiny bit of perfume on my neck, tuck the misbehaving chunk of hair behind my ear, and practically skip across the driveway to Anders's. Anders's younger brother, Jakob, answers the door and waves me inside, his mouth full of what smells like pepperoni pizza. Jakob is eleven but already taller than me and lanky like his brother.

Anders is on the couch in the living room, which is on the other side of the kitchen. His house is a complete mirror image of mine, down to the doorknobs.

"I told him to wait," Anders says, gesturing at the coffee table where two large pizzas are stacked, the one on top already short several pieces. His dark hair is wet, so the locks curl across his forehead, and he smells strongly of soap and freshly applied men's deodorant. He's wearing a tight white undershirt and a pair of red sweatpants spotted with bleach stains. I glance down at my own clothes, wondering if I misread the invitation.

"Stop it. You look nice," Anders says.

I stare at him. Did he read my mind?

"You still don't believe I can tell what you're thinking?"

I flush a little at that. If he knew what I was thinking half the time, he'd probably be embarrassed.

Jakob plops onto the couch next to Anders and grabs another slice. Anders hands me a paper plate and leans over the open box, inhaling deeply.

"Way better than cafeteria pizza," he says, lifting a piece so the cheese pulls.

I sit in the plaid wingback chair facing the couch and

watch him take quick, large bites like Giblet does when she thinks someone is going to take away her food. It makes me feel weirdly fluttery in my stomach.

"Get in on this," he says, and I load a piece onto my plate. "How are Cindy and Madison?" he asks between bites.

"They went home yesterday." He raises one of his glorious eyebrows, which lifts the wet locks curled across his forehead. I take a deep breath, debating where to begin. "Remember what Mr. Trappe said about Rachel being like a possessed doll?"

Anders puts up a finger to stop me. "Scram," he says to Jakob, who makes a whining noise. "Go watch TV in Mom and Dad's."

"Really?" Jakob asks.

"Yeah, but don't get anything on the bed."

Jakob grabs one of the boxes and disappears.

Anders brushes his hands on his sweatpants and then leans forward, his dark eyes on me, fully at attention even though his pizza is cooling on the coffee table in front of him.

"Madison tore Cindy's house apart a few days ago, and tried to do the same to ours on Wednesday."

"Wow. Whatever happened to her must have been pretty horrifying," he says.

"Yes. But I can't help feeling like it's not really Madison. Cindy thinks so too. And you heard Mr. Trappe. He thinks the same thing about Rachel."

Anders looks puzzled. "Who else could it be?"

I pick at a piece of pepperoni on my pizza. "You know the

play Mr. Kriska had me start reading the morning after she went missing?"

"Yeah."

"Well, I took it and read the rest. And there's an identical story there—a girl goes missing and comes back and her mom thinks her real child is still out there. In the play, we find out that magical creatures—Vila—took her and replaced her with a changeling."

He tilts his head to the side, more curious than judgmental. The outline of his jaw is so sharp I want to trace it with my finger. "But you don't actually believe that, do you? I mean, it's a play."

"I don't know what to believe, but I want to find out for sure, you know?"

"Okay," he says again. He seems worried, those thick brows meeting between his dark eyes. Behind him, I can see the woods. The sun is setting like a crown on the trees, haloing them in pink and gold.

"I saw the eyes again the other night. And I chased *it*— whatever it was," I tell him. "I didn't see anything besides a bird, but I feel like there's something else out there and I want to see if I can figure out what. I think it might be a wolf."

Now he looks incredulous. "You want to see if you can find what 'might be a wolf'?"

I nod. "If it was going to do something to me, it's had plenty of chances," I say. "I'm out there every night with Giblet. And if you come with me, there will be two of us. Plus, you're tall, so it's really like we're two and a half people."

He smiles, but I can see he's not totally into the idea. "I don't know, Luce. Are you sure I can't talk you into a movie instead?"

I shake my head. "You know if you don't come with me, I'll just go by myself."

"Fine. I'll get a flashlight. But I want my protest logged."

"Noted," I say. Anders pulls on a hooded sweatshirt that he cut between the ties so the neck is wider. He yells upstairs to Jakob he'll be outside for a bit and to call his cell if he needs anything. Jakob barks a reply, and we go.

I don't want to attract my mom's notice if she happens to be looking out the back windows, so we leave through the front door, loop around the far side of Anders's house, cross the lawn, and slip into the trees. The trees get denser as we move away from the development. The brush and ground ivies scrape against our knees and shins. The rabbit carcass is still there, and I can smell its rot.

"So, where exactly are we going?" Anders asks as we try to avoid a thorny bush.

"The last time I was out here, I found a clearing with a log in the middle and a lot of paw prints. If we can find that again, maybe it'll help."

I glance back at my house. Our porch lights are on, and I try to gauge a straight line to the log.

Anders uses his forearm to hold a branch out of the way,

and I pass under the arch he's made for me, close enough to smell a tang of sweat replacing his freshly showered scent. His hair is drying poofy, which I know he'll probably hate, but it's cute.

"There it is." I point to the fallen tree.

Anders brushes the log bark with the sleeve of his sweatshirt as though that will actually clean it, and we sit with our backs to our houses. I grip the flashlight and Anders holds his phone. It's past sunset now, but the sky between the branches is still gray and purple with only a star or two visible. At ground level, the darkness seems to settle close to us, slowly at first and then all at once. Anders fades into dusty shadow until I can't see anything besides the dark outline of his head and shoulders.

He takes the flashlight from me and shines it up his face, highlighting his chin and flaring his nostrils. "I just want to apologize," he says with a dramatic sniffle, mimicking a scene from *The Blair Witch Project*, which we watched a few Halloweens ago.

"Stop it," I say, snatching the light back. I'm already nervous enough without references to a movie where three teens hear sounds in the woods. My whole body is on edge, keeping me alert to every snap of twig and rustle of leaves.

"Was that a snake?" Anders asks after a shuffling noise.

"It was probably the wind."

Anders's fingers crawl over my hand. I freeze. His palm is covering the back of my knuckles, his long fingers curled between mine in a way that makes mine splay out. Is he scared and needing reassurance? Or maybe he wants to reassure me? Or . . . He squeezes, and I practically jump at the added pressure. I want to squeeze back, but I can't because of the weird position of our hands. So I slide the loop from the flashlight onto my wrist and pancake my other hand on top of his, like we're playing that kids' game where you try to keep your hand on top, sandwiching your opponent. I feel like my teeth are vibrating inside my head.

I try to blink the feeling away. We were children together. We invented fantastical worlds in these same woods—maybe even in this same spot. We saw each other with snot dribbling down our chins when it was cold out; we heard each other pee from the other side of a tree trunk; we squashed ant colonies; we drew on each other's skin with sticks and left red welts that we called tattoos. I've watched enough TV to know that this kind of thing between friends ends in disaster. But also, I have no desire to stop him.

Before too long, Anders slides his hand out of my hand sandwich and taps my knee. The soft sound of shuffling leaves moves toward us, quick like small running feet.

"There. That's the sound again," he whispers.

It slows, becoming quieter and more cautious.

Whatever it is, it knows we're here.

Anders taps my knee with one finger, then two fingers. Counting, I guess, but to what? Three? Five? I turn on the flashlight at three, and the beam catches a glimmer of yellow and then a fast streak of silver. A shoulder, a haunch, a tail? Anders grabs the flashlight, dragging me by the wrist cord, and takes off running.

"Wait, I'm stuck—"

I scramble behind him, but it's too hard to see the ground and keep an eye on the creature we're chasing. A vine or branch catches our ankles and we fall nose-first into brambles that prick my cheeks and arms. Anders groans. I roll onto my back, catching my breath, and look up through the branches. I can see the sky, still several shades lighter than the darkness around us.

He's laughing, and I can't help laughing too. I shine my light on him. Tiny red lines zipper across his face.

"You're as scratched up as I feel," I say, gently skimming his cheekbone with my fingertip.

"No! Not the moneymaker," he says.

I snort and roll my eyes.

A silence descends and we don't move from our place in the leaves, even though I'm pretty sure an insect is crawling over my hand. I open my mouth a few times—to say what? I don't know. I still don't understand completely what's happening between us.

"Hey," he says huskily.

My breath catches and my heart leaps. Is he about to kiss me? "Yeah?"

"Do you really believe all this stuff about changelings and the Vila?"

My heart dips. I stare at the dark masses of leaves, moving gently in the breeze. I decide to go with the truth. "I think I'm starting to. Anders, you should see Madison."

He's quiet for a moment. "There's got to be a logical explanation. Like some psychological response to what happened. Or—"

"I thought so too at first. Now I think something else is going on." I push myself up, brush off my jeans, and shake off the magic of the earlier moment. "I should get home. Weddings tomorrow and all."

"Okay," Anders says. I can't see his face or tell how he's feeling from this one word. I'm glad he can't see mine either, because I suddenly feel close to tears. There's so much beneath my skin—the disappointment about how this night ended with Anders, everything with Madison, and the fact that I'm no closer to figuring out what's really going on than yesterday.

We trudge back through the forest in near silence.

"Hey, Luce?" he says when we reach my backyard.

"Yeah?"

"I'll see you Sunday, right?"

"Yeah," I say. "We'll go find Mr. Kriska."

"And my party. Remember?" he says.

"Right. Of course." I cross my lawn. The motion light flips on, and I stare into it, letting it blind me. It's the only way I can keep the tears from falling.

24

LUCE

First Quarter (60% visible), Saturday, October 24

MIDMORNING, WHILE MOM is creating "beachy waves" for a bridesmaid, I'm listlessly working on homework on a footstool in the corner until I'm needed again. I withdraw *Picnic's Promise* from my backpack, where I've kept it since the night I finished reading it.

I reread act two, scene two, where the Vila mention the ritual that they complete during the full moon, to see if I missed something the first time. I didn't.

If this story is true, in one week, Madison will become Vila. I have a week to find her, to stop my family from losing her, but how? Waiting to surprise the creature at the log obviously didn't work, but maybe I can find a food or water source. There was a stream in the woods, I remember, where Anders and I counted tadpoles and caught snapping turtles years ago.

I have to try to find the Vila again.

We get home late afternoon—there are fewer weddings once the weather starts to cool—and my mom changes out of her work clothes. Usually she opts for sweatpants and a sweatshirt, but today she selects jeans and a floral peasant top.

"I want to check on Cindy and Madison. Do you want to come?"

I shake my head. If I'm going to help Madison—the *real* Madison—I have to go back to the woods.

Once my mom is gone, I grab some blue painter's tape and a flashlight, even though it isn't dark yet. I pass the log and weave farther into the trees, marking every few with a tab of tape. I follow some long-buried instinct, walking in what I think is a northwestern direction based on the sun's sinking position in the sky. I use a branch to haul myself up and over a fallen tree trunk that is crawling with termites, the bark a crumbling pulp.

I stop to listen. Distantly, I can hear a trickle. I take off in a jog, and soon, the trees thin, allowing in more sunlight. I almost skip right into the water. It is a much smaller stream than I remember, gurgling around green-slick stones and ducking under tree roots. I bend over it, my heels sinking into the wet mud of its banks. There aren't any tadpoles to count or turtles to provoke. I dip a pinkie in; the water is ice-cold.

I follow the stream until it takes a bend around a thick,

191

knobby tree. I step onto one of the mossy rocks to make my way around it, arms out to balance, eyes on my feet so I won't slip. When I look up, I see it.

A wolf.

It stands a few feet from me, frozen with its snout almost to the stream as though I caught it mid-drink. It is about the size of a large German shepherd, though it's rangy and more angular. Its gray fur is darker along the ridge of its back and almost white on its belly and along its lips. It's similar to the gray wolves on the sanctuary website, but there is something different about it too, besides the size—like it might be another subspecies. The ears are rounded and shorter than the ones in the photos I've seen, the snout stubbier, the shoulders and haunches broader.

Its golden eyes—ones I'm sure I've seen before—are trained on me, unblinking. The wolf is so still I may have thought it were a statue if it weren't for the tiny twitch of its left ear.

I crouch, reaching for a stick on the ground. When I stand back up, holding it high—though it certainly isn't heavy enough to do any damage—I find the courage to speak. "What are you?"

The wolf moves then, crawling so it is almost on its belly. It makes a soft *urrr-rrr* sound.

"Stop!" I yell, afraid of what will happen if it gets too close.

It begins to lengthen and unfold in front of me. Its legs grow, the paws sprouting knuckled fingers and toes. Its fur absorbs into the creature's pale skin. Its silver snout shortens and sharpens into a human nose. The space between its eyes widens and flattens. The ears curl into bare seashells. The tail disappears altogether. Before I can wrap my head around what is happening, there is a naked girl on her hands and knees in the water. My heart feels like it is thundering in my temples, the cold clamp of adrenaline along my spine.

She pushes herself to her feet clumsily, water dripping from her fingertips. She is much taller than me—maybe even taller than Anders—with a long heart-shaped face, a pointed chin, a slim-bridged, slightly upturned nose, and sharp cheekbones. Wild silver hair springs away from her scalp like a lion's mane but also hangs down her back in ropy locks. Her skin is brushed with dirt, but her muscles ripple beneath the grime. Despite her hair color, she doesn't appear to be much older than me; her skin is unwrinkled.

Then there are her eyes: They've changed shape, but they are still an otherworldly, glowing yellow-gold, giving off their own light rather than reflecting it. Twin stars sparking with energy.

I feel weirdly embarrassed by her nakedness, but also like I can't look away. She, on the other hand, seems completely unashamed, not wrapping her arms around herself like I would be if I were the one standing here naked.

I wonder if I fell and hit my head on a rock, if all of this is in my imagination. But I've never had a hallucination with all my senses activated: the setting sun lighting half her face, the stream babbling at her feet, a smell emanating from her—damp and musty, like the not-Madison's.

"What are you?" I ask, louder this time.

"I—am—Fan-ya," she says. Her words are slow and stilted.

"But *what* are you?" I say, still unable to believe what I am seeing.

"What?" she repeats.

"Yes, not who."

"Who and what—they are not the same? I am what I who?"

I shake my head, confused by this logic. "Are you a . . . Vila?" I ask directly.

"I know this word. The old ones use it." Fanya speaks English like she keeps it in a drawer and only takes it out on special occasions, fine china that could break at any second. "I am all forms," she continues. "Earth. Gray. Air. People. My heart-favorite is gray. What and who are you?"

"I'm Luce. A person."

"Luce, person," she repeats.

"Did you take Madison? The little girl with red hair?" I pat my head so she will know what I mean.

She flaps her arms like she is a bird about to take off. "Fox-furred small," she says. "Yes."

"Where is she?"

"In the teeth moon for the ritual."

I have no clue what that means. "You have to give her back!" I say loudly. Fanya flinches and backs away, wobbling a bit on her legs like a newborn calf.

I follow. "You took a little girl and her mother is so scared!"

"Her mother?" There's something about the way she says this word, like it's a precious stone.

"Yes. Her mother. She knows that changeling thing is not her daughter. Where is this teeth moon? Where is your den?" I realize I'm waving the stick and getting closer and closer to her, my heartbeat thundering in my temples. She takes another step back, her foot slipping on one of the moss-covered stones. She falls, her head smacking against a trunk.

"Oh no! Are you okay?" I didn't mean for her to get hurt.

Fanya shrinks. Her skin feathers and her nose sharpens into a gray beak. Her eyes become round like marbles, the yellow iris a slim ring around huge black pupils. A falcon—just like in *Picnic's Promise*. She flaps her arms again, and this time, takes off into the sky.

"No—wait! Please!"

Her feet tuck against the long fan of a silver tail. Her wings spread, the undersides a tessellation of brown and white arches. I drop my head all the way back to track her. She becomes a small speck against a darkening sky and disappears. My heartbeat slows, but still thuds hard against my skull. The adrenaline drains, leaving me feeling empty.

I take a few shaky steps until I'm clear of the mud and sink against a tree trunk. I feel like I'm going to throw up. Vila are real. I saw one with my own eyes. I spoke to it.

Vila are real.

Vila are real.

Vila are real.

I repeat the thought to myself over and over, but not even the repetition makes it feel less wild.

25

FANYA

I FLY THIS way and that so the Girl—Luce—can't follow me to our Den. The Den is where my Pack lives safe from traps. Where we curl into balls, coil into knots, and tuck our heads under wings. By the time I loop back to the stream to make sure I've lost her, she is gone. I coast over Luce's Den for People Only. There is light inside, but I can't see her through the glass.

The stream hid her river-pebble scent from me earlier. I would have run or changed to Air if I hadn't been so excited to see her up close. Her skin was hairless and plain. Her hair was the color of a beaver's pelt. And, once she was near, I could smell more of her too—a waxy smell from her underarms and something like flowers but definitely not flowers around her neck, right where I could see her pulse fluttering like butterfly wings under her skin.

She mentioned a Mother—Small's, who folded cloth while I snuck by. I wonder again about my own Mother. What was she doing when I was taken? Singing about apple seeds? What else do Mothers do?

I *fwup* back to our Den and land, changing to Gray. It is quiet, the Airs perched on Great Tree's hanging roots, the Earths asleep in a tangle. Even some of the Grays have returned from their dark prowls. I snuggle against Danica, my head on her warm belly.

"Mammaaaa."

I open one eye. The fox-furred Small is awake in the stick cage. I lift my head. No other Forms stir.

"Where Mammmaaa?" she cries.

"Be like dove," I growl, though it sounds like *Brr-Lic-Durrr.* And I guess doves are not always quiet, though they are always tasty.

"I want Mammmaaa."

Maybe the Small is cold? I leap over the cage sticks, grab her by the neck cloth, and carry her to our pile. She kicks and swings her little hands. One catches my lip and pinches hard. I whine until she lets go, shoving her fingers into her own mouth.

"Mammmaaa."

I curl around her and put my chin on her legs. She pats my head and grabs an ear. I am afraid she will pinch again, but she rubs my fur between her fingers. Her cries become whimpers, punctuated by little noises that made my ears perk. *Hic-cup hic-cup.* I lift my head and lick her face. *He-he-he-hic-cup.* I swish my tail, which makes her *he-he-he-he* again.

See? She can be happy in our Den. Someday, she will stop crying for her Mother. She will forget she had one, like I forgot. Eventually, she will learn to heart-decide Forms. She will *fwup fwup fwup* through the air or *sssss* through the weeds or chase rabbits. She will have a Pack, and that is a good life too.

WE WENT

WE WENT FOR the queen's daughter in the dark as we always had before. We thought nothing of the fact that the dwelling we breached was not a lone woodsman's cabin nor a farmer's cottage as usual, but instead a castle of stone. The babe was the queen's last, small and spindly, her hair like late autumn. Unwanted like the others, we thought, though she was wrapped in silk even finer than the pearl-beaded cloth the queen brought years before, and her cradle was lined with sumptuous velvet. We were already crossing back into our forest when we heard the queen's wails.

26

LUCE

Waxing Gibbous (70% visible), Sunday, October 25

I CHANGE INTO what I'll wear roller-skating—a schoolgirlish skirt that I never would have bought without Ashleigh's encouragement and a soft cotton shirt. It's a little chilly today, so I pull on an oversized sweatshirt I borrowed from Anders a few weeks ago.

When Anders honks, I grab *Picnic's Promise* from my backpack—in case it helps with Mr. Kriska—and canter down the stairs to the front door.

My mom emerges from the kitchen and stands with her arms crossed, leaning against the entryway to the foyer.

"Remember the rules," she says. "Which are . . ."

"Tell you where we're going and with who. Text you as soon as we get anywhere."

"So . . ."

I glance out the window. Ashleigh is sitting in the passenger seat beside Anders. The same bolt of disappointment I felt in the woods on Friday charges through me.

"We are going to finish research at the library," I lie, keeping my face turned away. "And then we're going roller-skating. Anders is driving me and Ashleigh."

She nods, satisfied, but I can tell by the way she's grabbing one hand with the other and rubbing her knuckles that she's still nervous.

Anders honks again when I'm outside, just feet from the car. I jump and he laughs, head back and hand on his chest.

"Hold your horses," I say.

"Whoa, buddy." He pats the dashboard.

"Hi," Ashleigh says cheerily when I climb into the back seat behind her. She's wearing a shirt she turned into a crop top and high-waisted jeans, her hair in a curled half ponytail. "Nice skirt."

"Thanks, I picked it out all on my own."

"Sure you did," she says with a smile.

Anders's eyes flit across the rearview mirror and catch mine briefly. It's too quick for me to glean any meaning from the glance.

Mr. Kriska's house isn't far from ours, but it takes a while to drive what is essentially a giant square around the forest to get to the other side.

He lives in a beautiful Victorian, painted a light grayish blue with dark blue accenting the shutters, fish scales, and roofing. The house has a turret, lead glass windows, and a long porch with spindle work and columns.

Made it to the library, I text my mom.

There is a heavy bronze eagle-head knocker on the door instead of a doorbell. I lift the head and knock, Anders and Ashleigh flanking me.

Even though it's afternoon, Mr. Kriska opens the door wearing a pair of white-and-blue-striped pajamas. It's a shock to see him without a sweater vest and khakis, or even his racquetball sweats. His collarbone pokes out of the wide V of the pajama neck, the cotton hanging loosely on his shoulders.

"Ms. Green, Mr. Knudtson, Ms. Arnett," he says as though he isn't surprised to see us. He glances down at what he's wearing. "I'm afraid I already dressed down for the evening."

"That's okay," I say. "Do you mind if we come in? I have a lot of questions."

He nods, moving out of the doorway to let us pass. The inside is as ornate as the exterior, with a staircase that curves back on itself and posts that have been carved with leaves and woodland creatures. A chandelier outfitted with fake candles hangs in the center of it all.

"Your house is beautiful," Anders says.

"It is," he says, looking around as though he's just noticing it for the first time. "It's been in my family for generations."

He leads us into a room at the back of the house that I can

only describe as a salon, with dark wood paneling offset by cranberry-colored wallpaper. The furniture is constructed of heavy golden woods, but the worn velvet cushions sag in their frames. The fireplace has a gray stone mantel, also chiseled into vines and leaves with small birds and chipmunks peeking out. Ashleigh admiringly circles a black grand piano in the corner.

"My wife, Samantha's," Mr. Kriska says, smiling wistfully.

An ornate chess set—clearly handmade—draws Anders.

"Can I offer you anything to drink?" Mr. Kriska asks, waving at three weary-looking chairs with floppy yellow cushions and delicately carved legs. Anders glances at them dubiously and then partially sits and partially hovers so the thing doesn't collapse beneath him. It holds Ashleigh with no problem. I remain standing, tracing the woodland creatures on the mantel, *Picnic's Promise* in my other hand. Mr. Kriska sinks into a dark chocolate leather wingback with brass hardware punctuating the ends of the arms.

"What happened? Why haven't you been at school?" Anders asks.

Mr. Kriska takes off his glasses and rubs his eyes.

"I was put on administrative leave," he says. "They're pushing me to retire."

"Why?" Anders sounds mortified.

"Because I wouldn't keep quiet." He looks at me. "I tried to tell them. Again. And again, the police thought coming forward meant I was involved. Of course, they can't nail that to the wall no matter how hard they try."

"You can't be the only one who has noticed that this happens before Halloween every nineteen years," I say. Ashleigh's eyes bounce from Mr. Kriska to me, surprised.

"Oh, people have noticed the disappearances all right, but everyone says, 'Oh well, the kids came back, didn't they? No harm. No foul.'" He brushes his palms together as though wiping away the problem. "That's Picnic for you. Sweeping real problems under a pretty rug."

Anders, in his undersized chair, shifts awkwardly.

"But the children who return are . . . different," I say.

"No one but the families wants to look at the reappearances too closely."

"Why not?"

He looks at me as though I'm naive. "No one wants to be labeled the town lunatic. 'There goes ol' Anton Kriska. Too bad St. Anthony's isn't still around.'" I allow myself a quick glance at Anders, who looks down.

"What *did* you see? Back when you were a teen?" I ask.

"I was in the forest hunting mushrooms." He gestures at the windows. On this side of the forest, the trees seem older, the trunks thick and gnarled. "I saw a snake crawling over a rock. A kind I hadn't seen before, so I tried to catch it, and it"—he pauses, looking up as though seeing something we can't—"changed into a bird and flew away. I spent every day after school looking for it again.

"I told everyone about it. My friends. Neighbors. Family.

That was my mistake. Not long after, my grandfather gave me *Picnic's Promise*. It's based on a family story passed down by my great-great-grandmother Robya. She's a character in it, you know?"

I nod, remembering the witch who tried to help Thomas because she was tired of how Picnic had treated her.

"Maybe if I'd read it first, I wouldn't have told anyone what I'd seen. I'd have understood that line about how Picnic can turn on its own. I'd have asked my father and grandfather about the troubles they'd faced with this town."

I take a deep breath because I'm ready to say something aloud, admit something beyond belief—doing the very same thing he did when he was young, risking the same loss. "I saw one too." I lock my gaze on Mr. Kriska. If I sneak a look at Anders or Ashleigh, I'll lose the courage I need to get this out. "Last night in the stream. A wolf that turned into a human, and then a bird."

His blue eyes widen and then grow glassy with tears. "You actually saw one?"

"Yes." I don't want to know what kind of faces Anders and Ashleigh are making. "She's been coming to visit the log behind my house."

He pulls a handkerchief out of his pajama pocket and makes a honking noise into the folds. "I've been waiting decades to hear someone say that."

"Mr. Kriska, do you know where their den is? I have to get Madison back."

He straightens his mustache and looks out the window again, at the expanse of trees. "I'm afraid I've spent my entire life trying to figure that out. All we have is what they say in the play." He points at *Picnic's Promise*. "Searching for a *great tree* that might be a den is like looking for a needle in a haystack."

My chest feels tight as we climb down the stairs and into Anders's car. This time, I take the front.

"You saw something last night?" Anders asks, his voice strangled, his eyes forward.

"Yeah. A Vila." I swallow hard. I know how it sounds. I've been resisting this truth for days.

"An animal that turned into a human," he says flatly.

"Her name is Fanya, and her pack has Madison."

Ashleigh shifts in the back seat. "Sorry, I'm still playing catch-up. I thought Madison was at home again, though. Right?"

I twist to look at her. "That's what Mr. Kriska was talking about. No one wants to look too closely. Well, I'm looking, and the thing that came home is not Madison."

Her mouth opens, and she breaks eye contact to stare at the back of Anders's head as though asking him for help.

"I know it's really hard to believe—I wouldn't have believed it either if it weren't for the clues," I say. "You know our research project on Picnic history? Well, I found out that a little girl around Madison's age has gone missing every nineteen years since the late 1800s. There's never any evidence of an intruder or a kidnapper. They all come back the next day. But their mothers know it's not them. Just like Cindy does now." I tick each similarity off on my fingers.

Anders makes a sound in the back of his throat. The tension in my chest feels like a rubber band about to snap.

"What?" I ask sharply.

"I never should have told you to talk to Mr. Kriska about seeing those eyes."

"Why?"

"I should have seen how vulnerable you are from all this. How open to—" He seems to be searching for a word.

"Suggestion?" Ashleigh says. I glare over my shoulder at her and she shrinks.

"You've had a confusing week," Anders continues. "So it makes sense that you're looking for answers that . . . aren't there."

I stare at his profile, but he refuses to look me in the eye. I know my real cousin. I *know* what I saw in the woods. And I realize how difficult it must be for Anders to wrap his mind around something this bizarre when he hasn't seen it himself, but I'm his best friend; he should believe me—especially when my cousin's life is at stake.

"Without Mr. Kriska's help, I wouldn't have known the real Madison is still out there and that the Vila took her," I say.

"Luce, he's clearly—" He pauses. Except I know what he means. It's the same thing everyone in Picnic has been saying for years.

"Say it." My voice is a low growl.

"Fine. He's clearly crazy."

The band snaps, sending a shot of pain to the base of my throat. My chest feels like it is rolling open, my heart blistering as it's exposed to air. "Let me out of the car." I pull on the handle, even though it's locked and we're still in motion.

"Luce—" Ashleigh starts, but I ignore her, pushing the unlock button.

Anders immediately locks it. "Luce, stop, we're in the middle of the road."

I push the unlock again. "No, *you* stop. I mean it—pull over."

He slows and veers onto the shoulder. I don't wait until we're completely stopped to fling the door open. "Luce. Come on. What about the party?"

"I don't care about the fucking party." His mouth falls open. I climb out.

"It might help to try to have a little fun," Ashleigh calls from the back seat.

I shake my head. "Not when my cousin is still missing." And I only have a week left to find her.

27

LUCE

I'VE NEVER HAD my heart broken before, but I imagine it feels like this—a searing sensation all the way down to your core that leaves you breathless. At times, I stalk in furious silence, replaying the conversation and trying out alternatives—what if I'd said this? Or that? Other times, I'm stumbling and bawling, emitting a sound I don't even recognize as human, the white line on the pavement dancing like a snake. I can't help imagining them at the roller rink, Anders showing off, skating backward easily with a dimpled grin while everyone else clip-clops awkwardly. Him spinning in circles, hands locked with Ashleigh's when they could be holding mine.

I pull off his sweatshirt because it smells too much like him—and I don't need any more reminders that I'm utterly alone. That my friends don't believe me. That no one except Mr. Kriska seems to understand the gravity of the situation and Picnic has all but erased him.

I tie the sweatshirt around my waist and realize I'm empty-handed. I must have left *Picnic's Promise* in Anders's car. Not that it matters. I doubt I'll find a clue in its pages given that Mr. Kriska has been searching his whole life and hasn't found one.

It's dusk when I reach our street. I wipe my face and pause. My mom expects me to be roller-skating, which means I have time to try to find Fanya again.

I stick to the far side of the yard, out of the motion sensor's way, and start into the forest, crunching over newly fallen leaves. I wave a cloud of gnats away from my face and start for the log. The path is easier now that I've been here before. I know which way to weave to avoid the tight clutch of brambles, the poison ivy patch that is knee-high, and the rabbit carcass.

When I reach the log, I circle it, trying to locate where the paw prints leave and approach the clearing. I crouch when I find a clear set, and use my phone's flashlight to trace it. It leads to what appears to be a low tunnel through the brush. I learned on some nature show that animals like to use the same paths over and over because it makes it easier for them to move between food and water sources.

The path is too low for me, so I have to make my own way beside it. The tree canopy transforms into inkblots as it grows darker, and the way ahead is difficult—full of ankle-tangling vines and leaf-filled valleys that are much deeper than they appear. At one point, I have to walk arms out, like on a balance beam, on a fallen tree trunk slippery with lichens. I wade through ferns that slice at my bare legs and the exposed skin at the backs of my hands. I really wish I weren't wearing this stupid skirt.

Suddenly, I stop; the sounds of trickling water catch my ear.

The trees clear slightly at the bank of the slim stream, arcing over it instead of crowding close. I think it's the same stream I visited last night, but I'm pretty sure I'm farther north from where I encountered Fanya. I shine my phone flashlight at the mud along the stream. There are so many prints here—all sorts of animals: birds, rabbits, deer.

A patch of dampened leaves shifts as though something is moving under it. A snake, I realize. It slides out of its leaf cover, amber with darker brown bands zigzagging down its back. Its head is triangular with a flicking red tongue emerging from the point. I don't know how to identify snakes, but I do remember my mom telling me that we have very few poisonous ones in Illinois.

There's something about this snake, though—the gold almonds of its eyes, I think—that makes me whisper, "Fanya?"

The snake slides in a circle as though chasing its own tail. It grows thicker, paler, and longer, moving faster until it creates a tiny tornado of dust. The column of dust grows taller and taller until a naked silver-haired girl stands in its place, her eyes flashing gold.

"You have to go," Fanya whispers. "You are too loud, and Nina hunts nearby. She may hear you."

"What will happen if she hears me?" I whisper.

"She might think you're dangerous to us—our pack. You are people only."

"What will she do?"

"I do not know, but she's our best hunter. And hungry. She eats the guts first while the creature is still alive."

I shudder. Behind Fanya, I hear a bird shriek.

"Run," Fanya says, the word a whispered bark. But I need answers. I need to find my cousin. I can't run away.

"Come with me," I say, reaching my hand out like when you approach a dog you're first meeting.

She shakes her head, but there is something in her eyes—honey gold in the limited light—that tells me she wants to.

"I won't hurt you, I promise," I say. "I just want to help Madison and her mother."

"Her mother?" She sounds curious.

I nod, and that seems to be enough. She takes a few fast steps and promptly trips. "How do you run with these?" she asks, gesturing at her bare feet.

Before I can say a word, Fanya falls to her hands and knees, fur sprouting down her spine and then spreading, nose lengthening, splayed fingers shortening, ears sharpening and rotating. As soon as she is fully wolf-shaped, she springs forward. I start sprinting, but I'm no match for her speed. She races forward and then loops back, making sure I'm still there, then races forward again. A pain shoots up my left side. My lungs feel like they will rip open, but I keep my flashlight beam trained on the bolt of silver.

She leads me back to the log via a path along the stream, which is much easier, though muddy. While I catch my breath with my hands on my knees, she stands up on her hind legs, transitioning from wolf back to human again. I watch her with fascination, but it all happens so quickly it's impossible to pinpoint the exact moment she is half of each. The long snout becomes furless as it grows shorter, and her body seems to stack itself, her center of gravity shifting backward. The hair on her head becomes coarser and longer. Even when she is all human, I think I can still see traces of wolf in her: the narrow, angular length of her face; the pointed nails on her fingers and toes; her body densely muscled, like all her wolf energy is coiled within.

I wonder what it's like to be able to transform. I feel so disappointingly limited.

She shivers.

"Are you cold?" I untie the sweatshirt from my waist. "Here."

Fanya takes it like she is in awe of the object and brings it up to her nose, inhaling deeply. She turns it around then, like she isn't quite sure how to manage it.

"Can I show you?" I guide the sweatshirt over her head and try to help her thread her arms through the armholes, but she starts to thrash, twisting in the garment. Eventually, Fanya manages to get the hood under her chin and one arm, backward, through a hole. "Just—just. Never mind," I say. I remember how she bolted when I started asking about Madison and her den, so I try to play it cool this time. "Where did you come from?" I ask.

"From?" she repeats. "I am from here."

"You've always lived in these woods?" I ask.

"Since I can remember."

"How old are you?"

Fanya shakes her head.

"You don't know?"

She shakes her head again.

"You look like you're not much older than me, except for the hair."

"After our moon blood, we stay the same—unless—" Fanya pulls the tips of her ears down with her fingers. She winces and lets them go.

"Unless?" I prompt.

"Traps," Fanya whispers, as though someone might hear her. I remember the silver chains the townspeople collected in *Picnic's Promise*, which strip the Vila of their ability to transform and render them mortal.

I don't know how much time we have, so I do my best to calmly steer the conversation in the direction I need it to go.

"Fanya, my family is scared. Is Madison safe?"

"She is at the den," Fanya says. "Safe."

"Where is your den?" I ask the question gentler this time, quieter.

She shakes her head. "I can't say. People only, they cannot know. Too dangerous."

I have to get this information.

"You are the one who took her?" I ask.

Fanya nods. "Teodora says our pack is too small, after"— she pulls on her ears again—"the two trappings."

"But why do you have to take someone else's children? Can't you just . . . make more?" I ask.

"Make more?"

"You know, the old-fashioned way." I flush a little at this.

"It is the old way," Fanya says. "The only way. The open-eye moon on Forefathers' Eve. Then the small grows into the power of forms so she can be people or earth or air or gray."

We're interrupted by a tinny melody, my mom's ringtone.

Shit. I forgot to text her. I silence the phone, but Fanya's body is already shrinking, her nose sharpening, feathers sprouting along her cheeks.

"No, wait. Don't go," I say. "It's okay. It's a cell phone." I hold it up and show it to her. She tilts her head and takes it with fingers that have elongated and softened. She pecks it with her beak-nose.

"It was my mother," I say.

Feathers fall away until she is fully human again. "Mother," Fanya repeats. She examines the phone closely.

"Yeah, on the other end. She's worried."

"What is 'worried'?"

"It's how humans feel when we care about each other. We get worried when the people we love are hurt or sick," I say.

Fanya closes her eyes. "I think I had a mother. Once . . . Do you think my mother worried?"

My body erupts in chills. Is Fanya one of the names on my list? If she doesn't age, it would be impossible to tell. I swallow. "I'm positive she did. What do you remember about her?"

She makes a strangled sniffling sound and palms at her ears. "An orange and a song about apple seeds."

I frown. It's not much to go on. "Fanya," I say, "Madison's mother is worried too. Very worried."

Fanya toddles to and fro in front of the log and makes a wheezing sound. I am afraid she'll either hyperventilate or transform again and fly away. "The old ones will not let me take small back," she says, clearly distraught.

"Even if you explain to them why?" I ask.

Fanya stops. "You mean, talk like people?"

"Yeah, talk to them. Convince them," I say.

"They don't listen to me."

"Will you try?" I ask. "For Madison's mother?"

Fanya makes a violent nodding motion, like something has loosened in her neck and she can't stop bobbing it. "Yes, I can try."

"Will you meet me here tomorrow night?" I ask. I need to stay in contact since we don't have much time.

"I will meet you here tomorrow night," she repeats, still nodding.

I smile, and her lips curl back as if she's trying to smile too.

"Goodbye, Fanya," I say.

"Goodbye, Luce."

28

FANYA

I WRIGGLE OUT of the cloth Luce gave me and dig a hole. The cloth smells sweet and clean like dandelion fluff, and I want to be able to dig it up later. It is a precious cloth given as a gift like in the stories the Old Ones tell, but I can't bring it to our Den. The Pack will know I have been with People Only.

At our hill, I hear Teodora chanting Old words. *Convince*, Luce said. Convincing sounds harder than talking, and I am not good with words. But I will do it so Small can be with her Mother, who worries. Because my own Mother must have worried too. And because I didn't get to know her, I can't remember her, and Small doesn't deserve the same.

When I return, Small is awake in the teeth moon, sucking on the dirty blue cloth she wears.

The Pack paces around Teodora in her milk-skinned People Form. *Fwupp*ing and *sssssss*ing and *huh-huh-huh*ing. I step over the teeth and lick Small's cheek. She tastes like salt.

"Doggy," Small says. "Good doggy."

Teodora stops chanting. "Fanya! You interrupt."

Small grabs my neck fur and clings to me. I feel something I don't know how to name—warm and sweet, like berries hanging on a bush on a hot day, but also something that makes my ears flatten.

"Fanya," Teodora says again.

I heart-decide People. Small makes a chirping sound while I change and holds tighter to my neck, so I stay on hands and knees.

"What are you doing?" Teodora asks.

"I must convince," I say, my tongue feeling even heavier than when I am with the People Only, like I have a fat juicy vole in my mouth. What words am I supposed to say next?

I push myself up onto my feet, wrapping my arms around Small. She rests her head against my under-neck bone.

"Small must go back," I say. "Her Mother is worried."

Teodora makes a sound: *heh-heh-heh-heh.* A few Gray Forms swish their tails.

"Many of us had Mothers," I say. "Who worried when we were gone. When we were taken," I correct.

Teodora makes louder sounds, stretching her lips back and grabbing her stomach. "What do we care about Mothers?" she asks. "During the first trapping in the Old World, Mothers baited us and sent their Men after us."

Teodora gets closer to me. The Small tries to bury herself in my neck.

"Has your Pack not taken care of you, Fanya?" Teodora asks.

I remember Danica, curling around me during ice days. Alina, play-chasing me. The memories give me the same warm-berry-ears-flat feeling I have holding Small. The Pack has given me Forms. Air Form, stretching and swooping. Earth Form, slipping and sliding. And Gray Form, which I love most, smelling and chasing and running and singing at the moon.

Teodora is so close, her squat People nose almost touches mine. "We are her Mothers now," she says, and I feel her tug on Small.

Small squawks, "No!"

But Teodora tugs harder. Small lets go. And I do too.

HOW THE QUEEN

HOW THE QUEEN and king from the castle of stone found out about silver, we shall never know. Maybe from the scholars' scrolls or the tales they sang. Or from the gods themselves—laughing on the other side of the veil at the chaos they designed.

The first trapping began when the queen and king sent their soldiers' and guards' wives to us, bearing cloth gifts like before, calling us sister. We didn't feel the chains until they seared the skin beneath our feathers, fur, and scales. They dragged us home, kept us as pets, hung us on walls. If they made the mistake of lifting our chains, our powers were restored and we ran. We grew smarter then, hid better. But the king's men set silver traps where we fed and drank. They surrounded our dens and lay in wait. There were too many.

We needed to escape.

29

LUCE

AS I PICK my way back to my house, I check my phone. *Double shit.* There are several missed calls from my mom, and a whole string of texts.

What was the one rule I gave you about riding with Anders? You're supposed to check in when you get somewhere.

Luce?

Then, ten minutes later: **Call me.**

Where are you?

Luce, answer me.

I enter through the front door so I can still preserve the

impression I'm coming from roller-skating—even though it's probably too late. I smell like forest: decomposing leaves, wood rot, earth.

My mom is sitting on the couch, the TV on but muted. One of her legs is crossed over the other and bouncing like a cat twitching its tail. Giblet races up to me, circling my ankles and wagging until I bend to scratch her chin. Anything to delay the conversation I'm about to have. I've never gotten in trouble for this type of thing, mostly because I've never had the kind of social life where I stay out late and lie to my mom.

"So my daughter doesn't check in to let me know she arrived safely at the rink," Mom says, her tone clipped. "She doesn't answer her phone. Or her texts. What do I do?"

The question is rhetorical, so I remain silent.

"I call the Knudtsons, who give me Anders's number. And you know what?"

Just the sound of his name feels like poking a fresh wound. I squeeze my eyes shut.

"Well, first he tries to tell me you're there, but then when I ask to speak to you, he tells me you went home after seeing Mr. Kriska."

I try to come up with an excuse, but my brain feels blank.

"Lying about where you were going aside, I know my daughter isn't home, she isn't at the roller-skating rink, and she certainly isn't answering my calls and texts. So, you might imagine every possible scenario going through my head: that you have been kidnapped, that you were hit by a car and are lying on the side of the road—"

"Mom," I finally interrupt. "Just give me a second to explain."

She uncrosses her legs and leans forward onto her knees, waiting.

I walk to the laundry room and grab the torn screen from behind the door. The screen is the only concrete proof I have right now, and even so, I know it isn't much. But maybe if she sees it with her own eyes, she'll believe it.

"What's that?"

I take a breath. "When I got home the other night, this is what the screen looked like. I found the kitchen window open and it was in the yard. Someone—or something—was inside our house."

My mom's V looks like it will merge with the bridge of her nose. "What?"

"Whether you admit it or not, something very strange is going on." My voice shakes, but I try to get it all out: "Food went missing from our kitchen. There are eyes in the forest. And Madison is not herself. Cindy doesn't think so either. I didn't tell you what I was doing because I thought if you knew, you wouldn't let me out of your sight."

She raises her eyebrows—a silent question.

So I answer. "I've been trying to find the real Madison."

She inhales like she's gearing herself up to speak, but she makes a small noise and stops. I can tell she's so flustered she doesn't know what to address first. Finally, she talks. "Are you actually using the disappearance of your cousin as an excuse for lying?"

I stare at her. Hard. Is she just going to ignore everything I said, like she's been ignoring what's really going on with Cindy and Madison? Maybe she's been brainwashed by Picnic like everyone else. But I haven't.

"I didn't think you'd believe me if I told you the truth."

"So you lied."

"I didn't have a choice!" I say.

"There's always a choice." Her tone is icy. "You're grounded."

I have never been grounded before. "So that means?"

My mom sticks out her lip and blows hair off her face in frustration. "You will take the bus to school and walk to the salon after. Nowhere else without my express permission."

"Sounds like my normal life," I say under my breath.

Wrong move, because she continues: "No going over to Anders's."

"Fine. Am I allowed to go to my room? Is that okay with you?" Without waiting for an answer, I turn and stomp up the stairs. I lie on my bed, staring at the ceiling. I feel an on-and-off pulse in my chest like a coin flipping, one beat fury, the other beat a deep, aching loneliness.

But if I feel all this, what must the real Madison feel? Away from her family, in some Den surrounded by wild beasts.

"I'm trying," I whisper to the ceiling. I wish I felt more confident, wish that I could say, *Whatever it takes, I'll find you.* How can I possibly do that now when I'm grounded and have no friends to help?

I only have six days left.

30

FANYA

AT GOLDEN LIGHT, Teodora wakes me. She slithers over my tail and flicks her own so I will follow. I stand, stretch with my haunches in the air, and shake the dust off my coat. Outside, she leads me to the stream and turns People. I lap water before turning too.

"Where have you been going at dark?" she asks, sitting on a rock and dangling her feet above the stream.

"I run and hunt like the others." I know enough not to say the truth.

"What?" she asks.

"What?" I repeat.

"You run and hunt what?"

"Squirrels. Rabbits. And food for the Small."

"Why don't you bring squirrels and rabbits back to the Den?"

"I do," I say. If I was in Gray Form, my fur would be up

between my shoulders, but I stand stock-still on my People feet.

"Not lately," she says. "I only see the People food. Fruits." She makes a scrunched face like when we eat rotten meat in the frost season.

Teodora skims the stream with her toes. I do the same. It is much colder with People skin. She meets my eyes with her own—a challenge. "The Small can learn to eat our food from now on. You are not to visit People Only," she says. "You are not to speak to them. You are not to bring them near our Den. Understand?"

"I would never," I say, dropping my eyes to my People feet with their tiny, fragile claws. "Never."

"Do you know what happens?" Teodora asks.

I think of the Old Ones' stories of being hunted, of how much bigger the Pack once was. "Yes, People Only trap us with silver and then keep us until we are bones."

"No. I mean, do you know what happens if we catch you talking to People Only?"

I shake my heavy People head.

"We will use our beaks to pull off your fur, your feathers, your scales. You will never come back to the Den."

My People skin feels tight and prickles like beestings. Where will I sleep without the Den? How will I hunt deer without my Pack? Who will I curl against when it gets cold? "What will happen to me then?" I ask.

Teodora lifts her shoulders and drops them again. "I hope

you don't find out," she says, and changes back to Earth Form. She drops off the rock, flicks her tail again, and slides away.

I heart-decide to be Gray and lie with my head on my paws. Gnats *zzzz* above the stream, dipping to the water and then back into the air. I failed to convince Teodora and now maybe she has convinced me.

Everything I know is my Pack. I can't lose it.

Can I?

31

LUCE

Waxing Gibbous (78% visible), Monday, October 26

I SLEEP FITFULLY and wake with my eyes stinging like I've been crying. I wonder what's happening to Madison right now. Can she sleep? Is she hungry? I doubt the Vila have Cheerios and 'nanas. Is she clean? She loves bath time. Cindy says she was born a fish, refusing to get out of the water until her fingers are well past pruney. The one thing I'm sure of is that she's scared—with only wolves, falcons, and snakes as company, how could she not be?

I get ready for school and go downstairs, feeling a bit like a zombie—bleary-eyed and stiff-legged.

"I'll pick you up at 3:30 p.m. sharp," my mom says. The salon is closed on Mondays, which means more time locked in my house like some sort of Rapunzel.

I ignore her, pull on my backpack, grab a granola bar from

the pantry, and slam the door behind me. Anders's car is still in the driveway. Since he's not sneak-picking me up, it'll stay there awhile longer, until after I'm on the bus.

When we pull up to school, Ashleigh is working on homework, but her head is down; I walk by quickly without a word. I get the books I need from my locker and duck into Mrs. Perch's room early. If I don't see Anders, I don't have to figure out how to act—whether to show him how hurt I am, or how angry.

I do the same at lunch, rushing to get in the cafeteria line so that I can carry my tray to the library. I take a seat at one of the study tables between the stacks where it's quiet, with only the occasional murmur of voices as students return or check out books.

I poke at the chicken patty on my tray. It's orange and limp and the gravy pooled on top of the instant mashed potatoes is the consistency of syrup. I push it away and open a map on my phone. Maybe there's a geographic pattern to the disappearances, and if I can find it, perhaps I'll be able to locate the den without Fanya's help. I drop pins at Cindy's address and the Trappes' house. I put Mr. Kriska's and my houses on it too. I try to find the two points along the stream where I met Fanya and make those pins a different color. It's still too few pins to mean much. I consult my notes, but I don't have any other addresses for the cases I found. It's unlikely the addresses from the late 1800s still exist anyway, at least not with the same street names and numbers. I need to go back to the microfilm and, this time, start with the more recent years.

I manage to convince Mom via text to take me to the public library after school since it's for my research project. It's a supervised visit, but she browses the fiction section while I ask the librarian to let me into the microfilm room again. Luckily, there are robust archives for 1982—with practically every week preserved—and I find this:

Jessica Turner, daughter of Lars and Brenda Turner, went missing from her house at 1165 S 235 on Oct. 15, 1982. According to police, Jessica was taken from her crib around 10:00 p.m. The culprit appears to have entered through the patio door, which was left unlocked. Police have yet to comment on whether they have any suspects.

"This is an ongoing investigation," said Police Chief Ralph Thompson.

The family reported hearing a noise at around 9:00 p.m.

"It was a *ssssss* sound," said L. Turner. "We searched the kitchen, expecting to find a snake or other animal."

Police did not respond to questions about the sound, but said that all possible angles are being investigated.

"We just want our little girl back," said her mother.

A press conference is expected in the coming days.

I locate the address and drop another pin onto my map. It's right at the edge of the forest.

I work backward again from 1982, finding a girl in 1963 named Corretta Heinrich, daughter of Daryl and Dana. There's no address in the article, but a copy of the white pages from the early '90s has a listing for D & D Heinrich. I'm not sure if the family moved or not, but the address is located near the forest like the others.

So far, the pins make a wide and imperfect backward C alongside the eastern edge of the woods, with my house at the bottom endpoint of the C and Mr. Kriska's on the top. Cindy's house seems to be the farthest from the middle of the shape, with a tract of farmland separating her from the forest. The two Fanya sightings sit low in the belly of the C. It makes me wonder if the Vila den is somewhere in the open space hugged by the letter. Even if that were true, it's still probably a few square miles' worth of trees. There's no way I could search that area on my own.

After we get home, I finish dinner and head up to my room to pretend to work on homework. In reality, I'm glued to the window. I don't see Fanya's eyes—no matter how I position myself. I press my nose against the glass, crouch lower, stand on my tiptoes, and angle my chin this way and that. Maybe the window is too high?

When I hear the TV go silent below, I flip off my lights

and climb into bed, fully clothed. My mom climbs the stairs and pauses briefly outside my room. I can see the shadows of her feet at the crack under the door, and I wonder if she's listening, making sure I'm still here—like so many mothers have throughout time. I feel a pang for my little cousin, and for Cindy, who knows that the child in her crib upstairs is not hers. She must feel as alone as I do.

"Luce, go to sleep," my mom says through the door, apparently attuned enough to my noises to know that I am, in fact, still awake.

Leave me alone; I'm fifteen, I want to shout back, but I remain silent, committed to my ruse, whether or not she believes it. I listen for the click of her door, then the sounds of her splashing in her bathroom sink, followed not long afterward by the groan of her bed frame as she climbs in.

I wait a few more minutes, then turn the knob quietly and sneak down the stairs, avoiding the creaky third step. Giblet is nestled in her bed near the refrigerator. She opens one eye and then closes it again, clearly deciding I am not about to feed her. I unlock the glass door and slide it back as slowly as I can. The *ssshhhh* of the door on its track makes my heart clench. I freeze and wait; the house is silent.

I step over the threshold and finally exhale. I cross my arms over my chest and curl my bare toes around the cold edge of the deck. Even from the back porch, I can't see her eyes.

"Fanya?" I call softly, hoping that her wolflike hearing is sensitive enough to detect my voice.

There is no response. She's not waiting for me.

It's possible she hasn't managed to convince her pack yet, or maybe she changed her mind. Or maybe she did try, and her pack is preventing her from returning. I don't know Fanya well enough to narrow down the possibilities, but I have a sinking feeling that I am not any closer to getting Madison back.

I glance over my shoulder. The house is dark and still, my mom hopefully asleep.

I cup my hands around my mouth and make the soft ghost noise: "Oooooo." I take a breath and try again softly. "Ooooooooooo."

Tick tick tick tick, the branches answer, counting down the days I have left to find Madison.

SOME HUMANS

SOME HUMANS IN the old world mourned the loss of the forest. They grieved the boar, now nearly gone from the underbrush, and hated the new king and his aggressive soldiers as much as we. One, a woman with skin like birch bark, gave us clothes and snuck us from the woods across the land.

We stayed in human form—our only safety. Our human feet, unused to walking, grew bloody and torn. Our skin, unused to wearing clothes, blistered and chafed. And still we followed.

The sea was unlike anything we had imagined: great and rolling green like a storm cloud. The sun was bright and hot, and we ached for the shade of our forest, the cool rush of our streams, the moon as white as ice. We didn't even have a chance to say goodbye to the only trees we'd ever known.

New woods lay ahead, the woman promised us. A new start.

32

LUCE

Waxing Gibbous (86% visible), Tuesday, October 27

WHEN I GET off the morning bus, Ashleigh is on the flower boxes, as always, wearing a pair of cutoff jeans with artificially torn holes at the knees. This time, she's looking up, as though waiting for me.

"Hey, Luce," she says.

"Hey." I'm wary. This is the longest we've gone without speaking, and I'm sure she and Anders have been talking about me.

"Any more news about Madison?" Her voice is gentle, and I suddenly want to cry. I don't know if the question means she believes me about any of it, but I appreciate her concern.

I shake my head, sure if I open my mouth, the tears will start.

"Anders had to run an errand inside." She indicates the school with her chin and then smiles in this way that suggests the errand might have something to do with me. I noticed his car was missing from the driveway when I walked by, so he must have come in early for it.

I cross my arms, feigning disinterest. "'Kay."

"You know he cares about you, right? He's really upset about Sunday."

I shrug at this. I need more than his care, more than his upset. I need someone who will stand beside me, especially when my little cousin's future is on the line.

"I'm here if you need help," she says. "If you want to talk or anything."

I try not to look surprised; I've always assumed she was Anders's friend first because of band and that I am more of a friend by proxy. But she looks sincere, her mouth puckered in a tight bow.

I nod in thanks, my jaw loosening. I didn't even realize how tightly I'd been clenching.

I open my locker before first bell and spot the brown leather spine of *Picnic's Promise*. This must have been Anders's errand: returning the play. I pull it from the shelf, and a notebook page falls out, the edges hastily torn. *I'm sorry*, it says in Anders's long, lax handwriting. He came in early and didn't bother to write more than two words? No context or explanation. Nothing about him believing me or not. I hold the note for a moment, not sure whether to laugh or to cry.

Whatever Anders's intention, I'm glad to have the play back.

I tuck the note inside and flip to act three, scene two, where the Vila mention rebuilding their den under a great tree—the same tree Mr. Kriska said he searched for. A few lines earlier, the Vila talk about rendezvousing at a hill. It's a long shot, but it's possible that the great tree is on the hill or, at least, nearby. I wonder if Mr. Kriska looked for hills too. We're on the flat plains of Illinois; there can't be that many.

I use my phone to search for a topographic map of Picnic and find one with contour lines representing elevation. There are a few rises in the woods, one of which falls in between the C's arms, north of my two Fanya sightings but still closer to my house than Mr. Kriska's. I drop another pin in my map, my heart thumping. It assumes a lot—that Mr. Kriska's grandfather didn't fictionalize this detail when he wrote the play, that the Vila haven't moved in over a hundred years—but it's the only clue I have.

I need to find a way to hike there while I'm still grounded. Daylight will make the task easier, which means skipping school again. I'll get in even more trouble with my mom, I know, but finding Madison will make it all worth it.

The app on my phone estimates how long it will take me to walk to the hill: two hours there and back. If I have someone cover for me at school, I'll have enough time to get to the salon at the end of the day and pretend like nothing unusual happened. Ashleigh said she was willing to help, and she's managed to fool the school before; I bet she'll do it again.

Can you call the school and pretend to be my mom again? I text. Tell them I'll be out the rest of the day for a family emergency.

Meet you in the bathroom, she texts back.

Ashleigh shows up a minute after me and we slip into a stall together. She chews at her cuticles nervously, but as soon as she dials, she transforms into the cheerleader I've seen at the top of pyramids: chin lifted, confident smile, steady.

"Ms. Baker?" She makes her voice deeper and bolder. I'm impressed; it does sound a bit like my mom. "This is Janice Green, Luce Green's mom . . . I'm keeping her home today for a family emergency . . . Yes, thank you for your concern."

"Damn. You're an even better actor than Anders," I say when she hangs up.

She laughs and shakes her head. "What are you going to do today?"

"Find the Vila who took Madison."

She looks worried, but she smiles. "I hope you do."

It's cooler out today than when Anders and I walked along this same road to join the search party almost two weeks ago. When the occasional pickup passes, I hop into the ditch and wade through the long grasses. I don't want to attract attention so some nosy Picnicker calls my mom at the salon.

When I reach the forest edge, I plunge in. I try to stay on the route, but it still takes me almost an additional hour beyond what the app predicted to reach the edge of the slight hill on the topographic map. The area doesn't seem noticeably different, but the ache in my calves suggests there's at least a gentle incline.

I watch the little bobbing dot on the map that represents me as I get closer and closer to the center of the hill. The trees grow spindlier—enough that I can see the slope of the ground. It's steeper than I thought. Ahead, there's a clearing, bald of trees and bushes, crowned with a single tree. It's the most massive tree I've ever seen, its silver trunk as wide as a car and scarred like the hide of an old elephant. Its branches are twisted and heavy, many dipping nearly to the ground. The knots and protuberances on its bark look like hundreds of eyes keeping watch on its kingdom of spindly subjects.

A *great* tree, I can't help thinking.

I almost break into the clearing, but something out of the corner of my eye catches my attention. A figure winding around one of the low branches. I squint. What I initially took to be vines are actually snakes, wound and draped like strings of pearls, on the tree.

I lower myself slowly until I'm on my stomach. Hopefully, I'm a lot less visible this way. I'm not sure how well snakes can see—or smell. I watch for a while, but the snakes are fairly inactive, appearing to sun themselves and sleep.

I glance at my phone. Given how long it took me to get here, I don't have much more time if I'm going to make it back to the salon by four.

There's a message from Ashleigh: **How's it going? We're worried about you.**

That *we* makes my heart skip a beat, but if Anders is part of that we, why hasn't he messaged me himself? Why couldn't he bother with more than a torn note?

I think I found the den, I text. I use the app to send my coordinates. **Doing a little recon.**

At the base of the tree, where one root lifts from the ground like a swimming arm, a triangular white head appears. The creature uses its front paws to drag itself forward, the long middle and broad haunches following until the animal can stand and stretch. It's the largest wolf I've ever seen—taller and bulkier than the wolves at the sanctuary and even bigger than Fanya. This creature has a whiter coat too, and its eyes are almost the color of marigolds.

Behind it, I can see the dark shadow of a hole or tunnel I didn't notice before.

The den.

I'm tempted to yell Madison's name or to spring up and make a run for it, but I can't risk it. I don't know how many more Vila are inside. They could easily catch me, and then I'll be another of Picnic's lost girls.

As I watch, a second wolf emerges from beneath the tree root, and I recognize the streak of darker gray along the ridge of the animal's spine.

Fanya.

It's the first time I've seen her in full light, and she's striking—her thick silver fur glinting in the sun. While she's smaller than the first wolf, she is more clearly built for speed, with long forelegs, powerful hind legs, a lean middle, and a tail that I can imagine streaking behind her.

Fanya seems to catch something on the wind. Her nose lifts into the air and twitches. Then she looks right at me. Her tail shifts back and forth, a subtle wag. Our eyes are locked. I feel a certainty in my bones then: she will come tonight.

I inch back from the hill, trying to move as quietly and slowly as I can. When I'm back in the dense trees, I take off running with way more energy and stamina than I ever muster in gym class.

I found the den. I know I can get Madison back. Now I just need a plan.

33

LUCE

I STOP AT a gas station bathroom on the way to the salon to brush the leaves out of my hair and return my skin to a pre-dirt state with a wet paper towel. Even with the cleanup, I can't help thinking I look like I've spent the past several hours outside. My cheeks seem ruddier, darkened by the late-fall sun. My gray long-sleeve T-shirt is a shade darker too, dampened by sweat.

I try to walk calmly and confidently into the salon. The baker who led the search party for Madison is in my mom's chair. She looks at me, like she's trying to puzzle out where she knows me from, but I smile blandly and quickly make my way to the back and drop off my stuff.

Cindy is folding towels in the back room.

"You're here!"

She looks a bit thinner than when I last saw her, the skin around her mouth lined and loose. She's wearing a wrinkled navy polo dress that renders her complexion a yellowish color.

Her hair, at least, is shiny, clean, and swept back into a loose ponytail.

She squeezes me weakly against her side. "Hiya, Luce. Want some hot cocoa? There are a few packets back here."

I shake my head but feel nostalgic for the winter afternoons I spent perched on the rumbling clothes dryer, fishing the tiny marshmallows out of a mug with my tongue. I hop onto the counter so I can sit facing her, and grab one of the towels to fold.

"How's Madison?" I ask cautiously, wondering if the changeling has destroyed any other rooms in her house.

"She's with her grandparents," Cindy says, avoiding my question. There's a bare spot of scalp right above her ear like she's been pulling her own hair out. Or maybe, something else has. She notices me staring and quickly tucks a loose strand of hair over it.

"Oh, is your mom in town?"

"No, her other grandparents," Cindy says.

"What happened to day care?"

"She kept trying to bite the other kids." Cindy doesn't meet my eyes when she says this, but her cheeks flush like she's embarrassed.

My mom is using a razor comb on the baker's hair, chatting about where the best apple picking is near Picnic.

"I think I know where she is," I say quietly. "The real Madison."

Cindy pauses in her folding and glances toward my mom's chair too. "Luce, I've been under a lot of stress. It's been making me anxious and paranoid." It sounds like she's repeating a script. Has someone convinced her of this?

"No, Cindy. She's out there, and there's still time to get her back."

Cindy shuts her eyes tight. One tear slides from the corner and down her cheek. She shakes her head hard. "Madison is with her grandparents," she says.

"No—"

"Please, Luce." Her voice is shrill. "I have to . . . get back to normal or I'll lose everything—"

I can't help feeling like someone is threatening her to change her story. Roald's parents? Her own? My mom?

Mom turns her chair to face us. She keeps chatting, but her eyes are glued on me. I slide off the counter, open the cabinet over the washer, and stack the towels inside.

With my back to my mom, I grab Cindy's hand and squeeze it. "I promise I won't let that happen. I'll find her and bring her back."

The corners of her mouth droop, but she squeezes back. Her grip is weak, like she doesn't have much energy left for holding herself together.

"What were you and Cindy talking about?" my mom asks casually as I dry the dishes she hands me from the sink. Giblet sits on my feet, hoping for scraps even though we've already scraped them into the trash.

I shrug. "Just catching up," I say.

"She didn't say anything about Madison?" my mom prompts. Her hair is clipped back from her face. The honey-colored highlights are bright, which means Cindy probably did them earlier today. That's very like her—willing to give no matter how she is feeling.

I shrug again. "That she was with her grandparents," I say.

"Okay. Good."

I put down the towel and narrow my eyes at her. "Why?"

"Mary Lou said something to me and I'm a little worried. That's all."

"Mary Lou?"

"Roald's mom."

As far as I'm aware, my mom hasn't said more than hello at the butcher's shop to Mary Lou. "Why have you been talking to her?" I ask sharply.

"She called me. She's heard a lot around town," she says.

"Like what?" I demand, ignoring the dish she is trying to pass me even though it drips right on Giblet's head. Giblet shakes and moves to her spot near the fridge.

"That Cindy's not fit—" Mom sets the dish on the counter but doesn't say another word. *To be a mother,* I finish in my head with horror. I wonder if Mary Lou is innocent in all this, or if she's the one planting the seeds.

I glance down at my hands, which have grown hot and red like lobster claws. "Do you and Mary Lou think that?" I ask, attempting to keep my voice from shaking.

"Of course not. We're trying to protect her."

I don't know how silencing her and forcing her to pretend everything is fine is protecting her. "Maybe what you think is protection is actually smothering."

"That's not fair, Luce."

I can't help thinking of Catherine and Emma, and even Rachel's mother, Linda. "Cindy *needs* us to believe her, Mom. We have to be on her side or something terrible is going to happen."

"I am on her side."

"Are you really?"

She's silent, but I can tell she's just biting her tongue—not that she's really considering my question.

"I have to finish homework." I leave her alone with the dishes and dump the contents of my backpack on the couch. I still haven't figured out how I'll meet Fanya unless my mom is asleep again, but that's still a few hours away.

I do homework with the TV on for a while, glancing up at the woods every commercial break. As soon as the local news comes on, Fanya appears outside: her eyes as yellow, shining, and steady as always. I glance at my mom, who is seated at the kitchen table, engrossed in filing her nails. I hold one finger up to the window and mouth, *Hold on.* I hope she understands.

Giblet climbs onto the couch to curl up beside me, and a

germ of an idea occurs to me. She loves to chase furry rodents. She's escaped a few times, but luckily, she barks as soon as the critter climbs a tree or dashes into a burrow, which makes her easy to locate. If I can get Giblet to bolt when I take her out to pee, I'll have an excuse to follow her into the forest. It won't buy me much time, but it's better than waiting until my mom goes to bed.

"I'm going to take Giblet out," I say, keeping the sullen tone in my voice so she doesn't grow suspicious.

My mom glances at the clock hanging over the armchair. "Isn't it a bit early?" she asks.

"I'm going to go to bed early."

Mom shrugs and goes back to filing her nails.

"Come on, Giblet," I say, patting my thigh. Giblet obediently hops down from the couch and trots to the door. I slide it open and she canters down the stairs to squat in the yard. I glance at the forest. Fanya's eyes are missing. How? They were there seconds before.

I step onto the patio and scan the dark spaces between the trees. Nothing. She's gone.

"Shit," I mutter under my breath, then slide the door closed behind me so Mom won't hear me. "Shit, shit, shit."

Giblet has finished peeing and is sniffing the grass, tracing a scent to the edge of the yard. I follow and give her a gentle nudge with my toe.

"Go," I whisper urgently. Giblet looks up at me like she doubts this will work.

"Go," I nudge her again. "You're free."

I glance over my shoulder. Mom is painting her nails now, leaning close over her hands, her tongue resting on her lip in concentration. I scoop up Giblet, holding her under my arm like a football, and step into the forest. I weave around trees, sticks cracking underfoot.

"Giblet! No!" I call for show, hoping my mom—if she can hear me—will think I'm chasing the dog. It's too dark to see Giblet's expression, but I have a feeling she is giving me the stink eye. I pull my phone out of my pocket and press on the flashlight, shuffling my feet to better feel the way.

"Fanya," I call softly, and then louder, for my mom's sake: "Giblet!"

It takes longer to reach the log with Giblet wriggling under my arm, but I get there. I sweep the ground around the log with the beam.

"Fanya?" I call again.

On the far side of the log, there are two divots in the carpet of decomposing leaves, the dirt beneath scraped like something slid or was dragged. There are another two divots behind them. The marks almost identical.

"Fanya?" I set Giblet down, gripping her collar, and squat to see the tracks better. Giblet sniffs them, her tail wagging.

"Is it her? Where did she go?" I ask.

Giblet drops onto her haunches and scratches an ear with her back paw.

"You're useless," I whisper to her.

I don't think Fanya would have left—not after whatever silent message passed between us earlier today and especially not after she knows I've seen her den.

"Luce?" I hear my mom calling from our porch. "Luce?"

"I'm coming! Giblet ran off, but I have her!" I call back, scooping Giblet up again.

I head through the forest toward our house. Giblet grunts softly and paws to get loose from my grip. I break through the trees at the edge of our yard and set her down on the grass. She runs to my mom and stands behind her legs as though I might try to football carry her again.

"Giblet ran off, huh?" Mom asks, the edge in her voice suggesting she doesn't believe me for a second.

"She did!" I pull a few leaves from my hair. "There was a rabbit."

"A rabbit?" She makes a show of looking at her watch. "Seems a bit late for rabbits to be out of their burrows."

"Maybe it was an opossum," I say. "I couldn't see it."

She emits a sound that is as much a sigh as a groan. "Okay, Luce." It's her *I'm disappointed in you* voice. I wish I could tell her that all of it—the sneaking, the lying—will be worth it if I find Madison and get her back to Cindy, but I know mentioning them will only ignite our fight again.

Upstairs, I pull open my bedroom blinds, checking for Fanya one last time. "Where is she?" I ask the trees.

They wave menacingly back at me.

34

FANYA

THE WIND DIES down and I can smell a mouse close by. I hop off and circle the log near Luce's Den. I hear a squeak from somewhere inside. I whine and paw at the bark. More squeaks. These even smaller: *squeak squeak squeak*. Is the mouse a Mother? I swish my tail, losing my appetite for the snack. I can't wait to show Luce the little mice—like pink People toes— when she finally arrives.

I don't know why seeing Luce at our Den earlier made me not scared anymore. Perhaps because she wasn't scared, lying on her soft People belly where any Air Form could see her. My Pack wants me to be scared. They told me stories of the Old times, but hid the truth from me. They took me from my own Mother. Just like I took the Small. They pretend to know what's best, but do they?

A twig snaps. I freeze and my ears perk. Luce? The air doesn't smell like river pebbles. It smells like the orange mushrooms that are shaped like People ears. Another twig cracks and a People Only steps out of the trees, with fur like corn silk, skin almost as transparent as a tadpole's. Has Luce sent this new People to talk to me?

I swish my tail and let the People Only get closer.

There is something hanging in the People Only's hand: a thick silver chain.

I heart-decide People, willing myself taller, naked-skinned, and safe from traps, but I don't decide fast enough. The People Only throws the chain over my ears as I try to change. It sinks into my neck fur, heavy like Great Tree's branches. I spin and snap and growl, but I am not strong in haunch, foot, or jaw anymore. I have been drained of everything except a weak flicker of life—a life that could turn to bones, to dust.

I cry like Small in our Den, ears flat and tail tucked. *Please,* I try to say. *Please let me go.*

The People Only drags me across the dirt.

WE LONGED

WE LONGED FOR the old world. The trees with black bark, the woolly-headed bison, the boar snuffling through the brush, and the women, with their gently embroidered cloths that smelled like their hearth fires, like their homes. We even missed the boys, song-struck at our circle's edge. But most of all, we missed their daughters, squalling and strong-willed.

In the new world, most trees were saplings, green-barked and young. The deer were wary and small. And the humans—they did not know what we could give, what we needed, what we took.

35

FANYA

THE PEOPLE ONLY with fur like corn silk puts me in a dark, airless part of his Den that holds a Night Beast. I circle it slowly. The Beasts are so loud—sighing and groaning down the hard gray rivers the People built. But this Beast's eyes are dim now, and it is silent and cold. Has it died? Teodora said People Only sometimes kill animals and hang their heads on the walls of their Dens. I hate to think of Danica, Alina, or even Nina's heads on some Den wall, their eyes replaced by shiny rocks. Could that happen to me too?

The People Only unfolds a cloth on the ground. I move so I am in the opposite corner and crouch, shoulder fur up. The silver binds me to this People Only until it is removed or I am Gone Forever, but it does not mean I have to be near him.

"It's for you," he says.

I growl.

The People Only goes away and comes back with a kitten

255

bowl of water. He sets it on the floor. My ears flatten at the thought of our stream.

"Come drink," he says.

I growl again.

The next time, he returns with something small and golden that smells like honey and grains. Food? I sniff the air; I can't help it. He holds the thing out on his pale hand. My stomach groans, so I snatch it and retreat behind the Beast. I crunch on the morsel. It is like nothing I've ever tried before—sweet and salty and hard and crumbly. It was a mistake to take it because now I want more. Teodora would never have fallen for a golden sweet-smelling square.

"Good girl," the People Only says. "You'll get more tomorrow."

Tomorrow? But who will feed the Small apples or invite her to the pile now that the nights are growing cool? And what will Luce do without me? She knows where our Den is. Will she hurt anyone? Or be hurt?

The People Only disappears. I stay hidden for a while in case he comes back, but finally, I can't resist the water any longer. I dart out and lap it in two tongues.

I perk my ears and sniff the door. I can smell more of the golden treats and other smells too: pig meat, tubers, garlic. I paw at the wood, but it does not open.

On the other side of the dark room, there is another door that takes up the whole wall. Through the crack at the bottom, I smell grass and fallen leaves. That is the way to freedom, but that door is even stronger than the first.

I scrape at the chain around my neck with my back paw and try to chew at the silver, but the metal burns my gums and tongue. It is Old magic, Teodora says. Older than her. Older than our rituals. From the time of Baba, the bestower of fate. I am no match for something so old.

The cloth smells like the People Only; I drag it under the Beast's cold belly and curl up. From there, I can see both doors. There is nothing to do now but wait, ears flattened, fur up.

36

LUCE

Waxing Gibbous (92% visible), Wednesday, October 28

I'M AWAKE LONG before my alarm, flipping through
photos on my phone. I stop at one of Madison at the bottom
of a slide grinning up at me, a few small teeth poking from
her lower gums. She has a bow on her head, but most of her
hair has fallen out of the tie and formed a feather-soft red halo
around her face. She looks so happy it hurts.

Without Fanya's help, I'm as alone as ever in trying to rescue
her. I don't know how many Vila are in the den. Nor do I know
how Madison is being guarded. There are too many variables.
The only thing I know is that silver is the Vila's weakness.

I wait until my mom goes down to make coffee and let out
Giblet, then I slip into her room. She doesn't wear much jew-
elry, but she keeps a few items. I open the wooden box on her
bureau. There's a nice chain with a pendant that is, at least,

silver in color, but I have no way of knowing if it's made of white gold or nickel or some other metal. I pocket it anyway and text Ashleigh: **Do you have any silver necklaces?**

No . . . but my mom probably does. Why?

Think you could "borrow" one for me?

It's important.

Ok. She probably won't notice.

I hope she's right.

It's cool enough today that I wear a canvas jacket on my walk to the bus. I have my headphones in and am listening to music to hide the fact that Anders's chatter isn't filling the silence. I don't hear his car tires crunching gravel until he pulls up beside me. I pause the music but keep my headphones in. Anders leans his whole head out the window, like a dog on a car ride.

"Hey, did you get my note?"

I pretend I can't hear him. It's childish, I know.

"Luce. Luce."

That's my name. Don't wear it out, we used to say to each other as kids. "What?" I snap.

"Did you get my note?"

"Yes."

"And . . . ?" I don't know what he expects me to say. It was a two-word apology. No explanation. No recognition of how he hurt me.

"And . . . ?" I repeat.

"Please get in so we can talk."

I ignore him.

"Fine," he says, and I expect him to peel off, but he stays beside me, inching forward at what is probably two miles per hour. "I'll just keep you company."

He turns on the radio, switching stations until he finds an early '00s station playing Kelly Clarkson's "Miss Independent." "Miss independent. Miss self-sufficient. Miss keep your distance," he sings. I don't even have to look at him to know he has a big cheesy grin on his face. If I keep ignoring him, he'll become an even bigger ham, performing because that's the only way he knows how to get people to like him. "Come on! Remember I can tell when you're not really mad? That cheek muscle gives you away," he says.

That's it: the flint I need. I spin, practically sputtering: "Then I guess you don't know me or my face very well!"

"Whoa. Whoa. I said I was sorry!"

"For what? Do you even know?"

He puts the car in park and climbs out, positioning himself in front of me. I sidestep him and keep walking. He shuffles to keep up and pushes his hair back with both hands, something he only does when he's trying to compose himself. "I read the play."

That stops me. I cross my arms and wait, feeling more like my mother than I'd ever admit out loud.

"You have to understand that this is all a lot to take in. I mean, babies who aren't the babies they look like? Wolves who are women and birds and snakes?"

"So what are you saying—do you believe me now?" I think of Catherine, of Emma, of all the women who lost their children and weren't believed. "No matter how wild the story, do you believe me because I'm your best friend and I wouldn't lie to you about this?"

He hesitates—just a fraction—but it's too long. I feel the sear in my chest again.

"I believe you, but I don't know if I believe in *it*," he says, as though this is some great distinction.

I turn on my music, volume up, and start down the road again. This time, he doesn't try to stop me.

After school, I walk to the salon, Ashleigh's mom's necklace in my pocket beside my mom's. I still don't have a plan. I've been over and over what I know about the Vila all day, and my only resource, as far as I can tell, is Mr. Kriska. If he plays racquetball with that kind of strength, maybe he can hike into the woods with me and—and what? Burst into the den with two necklaces? I'm still not sure, but maybe he'll have ideas, if only I can talk to him again.

Both Cindy and my mom have clients when I arrive. Cindy has her hair down and combed over to the side. To cover more bald spots? She smiles weakly at me in the reflection and my mom, characteristically, assigns me chores in a clipped tone.

We're in the midst of an only-talking-when-necessary standoff. Near 5:00, she calls me over to her chair.

"I still have another two clients," she says. "Cindy is going to take you home after she picks up Madison. I want to see you doing homework when I get there."

Cindy is quiet in the car. She's always had a bit of a lead foot, as my mom says, but she's driving slowly today, almost as though trying to delay the pickup.

We pull up to what I assume is Roald's parents' house, and she leaves me in the car. I watch her pause at the bottom of the steps up to their door, seeming to gather herself. She emerges a few minutes later, holding the not-Madison against her hip, facing outward. Not-Madison's legs are stiff, banging against Cindy's thigh, and her head hangs down over one of Cindy's arms. Cindy grunts as she hauls not-Madison into the car seat and tries to buckle around the stiff limbs. There are tiny ripples on not-Madison's skin now, like her seams are starting to show. I turn back around, glad that she is, at least, contained.

Cindy climbs back into the driver's seat, her hands trembling as she attempts to turn the car back on. I realize this is my chance.

"Cindy, can you take me somewhere else? There's someone who I think can help with—" I gesture behind me, unwilling even to call her Madison's name.

Cindy shakes her head. "Your mom told me you were grounded. She would kill me."

"If she finds out, we'll blame it all on me. She can't kill me. I'm her offspring."

Cindy smiles a little at that. She used to have a big-toothed grin, but I realize I haven't seen it once since this all happened.

"Can you really keep doing this? Every day?" I ask.

She looks in the rearview mirror and shudders. "No."

"Then take me. I promise I'm getting close."

Cindy pulls up Mr. Kriska's driveway and angles her neck to see the full house better. The porch lights are on and a wind chime tinkles quietly in the breeze.

"Wow," she says. "This is Mr. Kriska's house?"

I nod. "He's the one who helped me figure this all out. Do you want to come in?"

"I better stay with her—in case—" Cindy doesn't finish the sentence, but I can imagine: in case she chews through her car seat straps, in case she destroys the car, in case she runs wildly into the night and eats someone's pet dog.

I ring the doorbell. The curtains beside the door shift and there's a long pause. Mr. Kriska opens the door a crack, peering through it at me. I catch a glimpse of his khakis and sweater vest, which is reassuring. Maybe things are going back to normal for him.

"Ms. Green." His voice sounds tight and nasally. He doesn't open the door any wider. I try to peek behind him without looking like that's what I'm doing. Does he have company? "I was just about to go out," he says.

"Oh—I'm sorry. It's just that I found the den, and I need your help rescuing my cousin."

The door swings open wider, and I step inside the foyer. We're lit by the chandelier, but the rest of the house is dark. I can hear a clock ticking from the shadows. "Where?" he asks eagerly.

I open my mouth to answer, but I notice that his forehead is damp with sweat and his eyes, overmagnified by his glasses, are too wide. Wild even. "Is something wrong?" I ask.

"No. Nothing," he responds quickly.

"Okay . . ."

"You were saying about the den," he says.

Something in my gut is tugging at me, telling me this situation is off. Again, I sidestep the question. "The Vila that was going to help me get Madison back is gone," I say. "Something got her, I think. And I was hoping—"

There's a soft whimper, somewhere deep in the house. He glances behind him and then back at me. The sweat on his forehead beads.

"Do you have a dog?" I ask. I don't remember seeing one last time.

"Yes," he says quickly. "Samantha loved dogs."

The whimper gets louder, and then transforms into a mournful howl. The hair stands up on my arms. I can't help thinking I'm hearing my name.

Lu-Lu-Luuuuuuu. Lu-Lu-Luuuuuuu.

I follow the sound, walking through the foyer into the shadowy corridor that leads, I think, to the kitchen.

"Ms. Green—" Mr. Kriska says, hurrying after me. "Ms. Green—" He steps into my path, one hand planted on each side of the hallway. I take a step closer, but he doesn't budge. He's not a large man, though I don't think I'm the type of person to push my way in.

Lu-Lu-Lu-Luuuuuuu. I know that howl.

"Did you take her?" I ask. "The Vila I met behind my house. The one I told you about. Fanya?"

He closes his hands into fists and seems to be pushing outward on the walls. At first, I think he'll lie, but he levels his chin. "Yes. I have her. I need her."

"You need her?" I echo.

"They think I can't do my job anymore. I have been laughed at for too long. Those cops the other day—" He shakes his head like he can't even bear to face the memory. "Now that I have proof, I will show them. All of them."

He's captured Fanya so that he can restore his reputation? I'm not convinced it will work. If reading about the missing girls has taught me anything, it's that Picnic can hide from what is right in front of its face if it wants to. "Mr. Kriska, she's going to help me get Madison back," I say. "I don't know enough about the Vila to do it on my own."

"Don't worry about that. Once I show the town what she is, they'll all help. You'll have an army of people knocking down the den." His arms are shaking, despite his planted fists. I never would have pegged him as an angry man, but I think about all that's happened. My best friend not believing me. My mom refusing to listen. A town spreading rumors about my aunt. I've felt hurt and angry, and that was only a few days compared to a lifetime of it. Still, I can't help seeing one similarity.

"You sound like the mayor," I say. "In *Picnic's Promise*."

He drops his hands then. I see my window.

"There must be a reason your grandfather wrote that play and gave it to you—a reason the story was passed down from your great-great-grandmother," I say.

I'm fishing, but he seems to be looking through me, remembering something. He nods.

"You said you wished you'd had it earlier so you would have known how Picnic turns on its own. But what if the reason you were given it has to do with the father, Thomas?"

He rubs his knuckles and tilts his head to the side. "Thomas failed."

I shake my head. "He saved some of the Vila, even though he'd been hurt by them."

"But they still didn't give his daughter back."

"You're right. I think it was too late for her. But it's not too late for Madison. We have until Saturday." A thought occurs to me. I beckon him back down the hallway and through the foyer toward the front window. I push aside the curtains so he can see Cindy. She has the overhead light on and she's twisted

266

around in her seat, and though we can't tell what she's doing, I'm sure it involves trying to distract the not-Madison from something destructive.

"That's my aunt, Cindy. I think you might remember her. You were her teacher."

He straightens his glasses. "Yes, I remember."

She turns back around and hugs the steering wheel with her arms, resting her chin on top. In the overhead light, her skin and eyes shine, clear and bright, like she's a Madonna figure, a mother for all mothers.

"This is crushing her, Mr. Kriska. Please."

He tugs at one of his oversized ears.

"What would Samantha have wanted?" I ask. I didn't know his wife at all, so it's a gamble based on Mrs. Griswald saying she was kind. But it works.

He turns stiffly and leads me down the hallway, through a butler's pantry, into the kitchen, and to a door on the far wall.

A station wagon sits in the middle of the garage. Fanya is there, her gold eyes flashing in the dark. I flip on the light and she backs into the corner, hanging low to the ground, the nearly black fur between her shoulder blades and along her spine rising. A silver chain glints around her neck.

She growls under her breath, a deep *eeeeerrrrr*.

"Maybe it would be better if you waited inside," I tell Mr. Kriska, who steps out of the doorway.

"Fanya, it's okay. I'm here." I put my hands up and approach her slowly. She stops growling, but remains shrunken in the corner, like she's trying to disappear into the wall. When I'm close enough, I reach for the chain and slide it off, tucking it into my pocket with the necklaces. "You're safe now," I say.

Removing the silver frees Fanya immediately. Her shoulders drop, the fur flattening until it becomes bare skin, prickled with goose bumps, and an aura of frizzy flyaway hairs forms around the crown of her head. The rest of her hair curtains her long narrow-heart face and almond-shaped eyes. There is a tiny red welt on her neck where the silver was. She's crouched on her hands and her knees, her fingers splayed for balance.

I pull off my jacket. "I'm going to put this on you, if that's okay." I gently drape it over her shoulders like a cape. She flattens herself against her knees as though the weight of it is too much. I don't think she'll want to go back through the house, especially with Mr. Kriska inside, so I hit the garage door button. It lifts with a groan. Fanya winces at the sound, and then, seeming to understand she's free, spider crawls, jacket perched on her shoulders like fly wings, and squeezes through the widening crack at the bottom.

I follow. On the other side of the door, Fanya gets to her feet and wobbles like she is stepping on sharp stones down the driveway. The crickets chirp madly all around her as though applauding her freedom.

37

LUCE

I LEAD FANYA to Cindy's car, and my aunt climbs out, probably startled by the nearly naked girl lit by her headlights.

"What's going on?"

"Cindy, this is Fanya. She's—" I pause. Telling Cindy what she is is a long story, especially when Mr. Kriska is still inside and could change his mind about Fanya any minute. "She knows where Madison is."

Cindy's phone rings and Fanya backs up behind me at the sound. "Shit. It's your mom," she says.

"Tell her we went to your house so that I could watch Madison."

I must seem desperate enough, or she's too bewildered by what is happening to protest. She picks up the phone, stepping a few feet away so she can talk to my mom.

I open the back door. Fanya curls her lip at the not-Madison, who growls back.

"Please get in," I say. "We can go back to Cindy's so you can rest, and we can make a plan to get the real Madison back."

"I do not like the night beasts. They are loud and smell." I look at Cindy's small hybrid in confusion. It's much quieter than most cars.

"I understand, but it's the fastest way."

"Faster than air form?"

"Probably not, but Cindy and I can't fly."

She climbs in with a glare, and I try to buckle her, but she arches her back like when Madison fights her car seat.

"It's to keep you safe," I tell her. "There's no silver."

But she snaps her teeth at my hand like she's still in wolf form, so I drop the belt. She pushes herself into a squatting position, facing the window instead of not-Madison, arms wrapped around her shins, chin resting on her bony knees. I drape the jacket over her again and climb in the front.

"Fanya, are you hurt?" I ask gently as Cindy backs out of the driveway.

She doesn't respond.

"I'm so sorry this happened to you," I try again.

She seems to ball herself more tightly under her jacket shell.

"You can trust us. I promise," I say. "We're not like him."

"Teodora says people only can't be trusted."

Cindy glances in the rearview mirror. "You're right about that," she says.

I shoot her a look, but she shrugs. "After the kind of week I had, I'm not feeling too hot about them either."

"The pack is no better. The old ones will tear my feathers and scales if I go back," Fanya says.

Cindy looks at me, alarmed. I sigh and tell her what I know about the Vila. I leave out the part about Fanya being the one to actually kidnap Madison. Every time I pause, Cindy swallows, like she has to try to keep the story down.

"So they are the ones who made . . . that." Her eyes dart to her rearview mirror.

I nod.

Unlike the others I've told all or portions of this story to, Cindy doesn't protest about how impossible it is, perhaps because she has already come to grips with something unbelievable right behind her—the not-Madison hissing at Fanya.

At her house, Cindy carries not-Madison upstairs to the crib, promising to return with some clothes that might fit Fanya.

Fanya approaches the photo of Madison on the side table before backing off and then approaching it again—just like Giblet when she finds a possum in our backyard.

"That's a picture of Madison," I say. "Like a copy."

"Small," she says softly.

"Fanya, I'm very worried about Madison. I'm guessing you weren't able to convince your pack to let her go."

"No. I tried but they did not listen." She palms at her head like a baby with an ear infection. "People only trap the pack.

271

The pack takes people only. Neither is good. So why does it matter where Small grows up?" Fanya says.

"She's why," I say, just as Cindy descends the stairs, holding some sweatpants and a sweater that I'm sure will be much too small.

"A mother."

"A mother who is good and true and loves Madison very much," I say.

Cindy sets down the clothes on the couch, and Fanya brings the sweater up to her nose.

"Sheep," she says.

Cindy nods. "We call it *wool*. Can I help you put it on?"

Fanya allows her to slide my jacket off her shoulders and pull the sweater on. This time, she doesn't fight the armholes and manages to get her hands through the sleeves. Once dressed, though, she keeps shrugging like she wants the clothing to stop touching her. It's too short too, falling mid-shin and mid-forearm.

"Itchy," she says.

"It can be," Cindy says with a smile.

"Why do you wear it?"

"Because it's also warm," I say.

Fanya looks dubious.

"Are you hungry?" Cindy asks.

Fanya nods.

"What do you like to eat?"

"Deer. Rabbit. Squirrels. Oranges. Gold grain squares."

"Hmm. I'll see what I can find," she says.

I point to the couch. "You can sit if you want."

Fanya pokes at it with a finger, and then sits. As soon as she sinks in, she pops up again as though surprised by its softness. She squats on the floor instead, tugging at the fabric of the too-short pants.

Cindy emerges from the kitchen with a glass of water and plate of shredded rotisserie chicken. She hands her the glass and Fanya grabs it with both hands and cocks her head to the side. I mime drinking it for her, but she tilts it too far, dribbling it down her chin and chest. She frowns and laps at the remaining water in the glass instead.

Cindy sets the plate on the coffee table beside Fanya. Fanya flaps her arms and plants her face in the plate. She manages to get a mouthful and then tilts her head back, like she wants it to fall to her back molars so she can chew.

"Wait. Use your fingers," Cindy says, getting on her knees in front of Fanya. She takes a piece of chicken and puts it in her own mouth. Fanya grabs a piece with her hands and does the same. It reminds me of when Madison started eating solid foods. She squeezed the food into fists and then shoved them toward her mouth, often missing completely. By the end of a meal, I had to hold her over the sink and scrub her cheeks and forehead to get her clean.

Fanya shakes her head at the finger method. "Not as fast,"

she says, and dives mouth-first into the chicken pile again.

Cindy laughs. "You're right, I suppose."

I smile at her, kneeling eye to eye with Fanya too. It's nice to see Cindy laughing and making jokes after all that has happened the past two weeks—even though Madison is gone. Because at least now she knows the truth.

THERE WERE BATTLES

THERE WERE BATTLES to be fought in the new world too. Men who needed looking after. We fought as before, strong and fast and true, and, later, as the Forefathers' moon approached, took our prize: a raven-haired babe with strong lungs and eyes like wheat. She was the only in her household, but exceptions must be made for the survival of the pack.

They do not know the old ways here, and, still, the betrayal was like before, our silver secret traveling across even an ocean. They shook their chains and set their traps a second time. They roared in our quiet glens: How dare you! We are men! These are our children!

They wanted the victory and the spoils.

We wanted to survive.

38

FANYA

LUCE'S MOTHER COMES for her in a Night Beast that makes a terrible honk, like an injured goose.

"I'll be back with a plan," Luce says. "In the meantime, please stay here and do what Cindy says."

I follow the fox-furred Mother as she retrieves the Leftover from the baby cage and brings it back down. She seats it, ties it across the belly and chest, and puts a flat white surface in front of it.

She puts a metal container under a snake that spouts water. Then she places it on a black coil and starts a fire beneath it. I watch, amazed.

"Are you still hungry?" she asks. Her eyes are like the stream cutting around rocks on a sunny day.

I lick one of my fingers, still shiny with chicken skin oil, and bob my head.

A little while later, she uses a claw-shaped object to scoop what looks like yellow worms onto the flat white surface for the Leftover and onto a round slab for me. I sniff the worms, remembering the burnt-cow smell the night I snuck in. I touch my tongue to one. It's salty, like all People Food, and I love it immediately.

"Noodles," she says. "With butter." She shows me all her teeth. I'm learning that, in the People world, this is like a tail thump. I try to show my teeth too.

She winds the noodles around a metal object with three spikes and sticks it in her own mouth. I slurp at them, so they flap against my chin. Then slurp some more. The noodles are slick and slide down my throat easily.

The Leftover squishes the noodles in its fist and flings them. The fox-furred Mother pretends not to see.

"Is Madison okay?" she asks. "Is she getting enough to eat?"

I bob my head up and down. "Apples. She makes a *he-he-he-he* sound." I mimic it.

She looks down. "I just want her to be happy and safe." Her voice does something funny then, like there's a bone stuck in her throat.

I paw at my ears. I didn't know I was missing anything until I stepped into this Den the first time to take the Small. And now I can't stop the questions in my head. Did my Mother have stream eyes that made you want to dive in? Did she make food over a fire? Did she show all her teeth? I wish I could see more of her than a shadow in a foggy memory.

277

"I think I was taken when I was a Small too," I tell her.

"Oh God. That's awful. Have you tried to find your parents?"

I shake my head. "I don't remember them."

The Mother puts down her noodles and folds her arms around me. I freeze. Does she have silver chains? Mothers can trap too, Teodora says. No, I remember I am safe in People Form.

The smell of lavender on her makes my muscles go soft, and it is warm against her, like our sleeping piles in the Den.

"I'm so sorry," the Mother says. Water falls down her face, and I want to lick it away. I wonder if my own Mother wasn't fooled by the Leftover put in my place. If water fell down her face. If someone folded her in their arms.

"I'll help get Small back," I tell her. I wish someone had told my Mother the same.

39

LUCE

Waxing Gibbous (96% visible), Thursday, October 29

I FELL ASLEEP trying to puzzle out how Fanya and I can break into the den to get Madison. I wake up thinking about it too, and suddenly, in the pale-yellow glow filtering through the slats of my blinds, it seems obvious: a bait and switch. Fanya could carry the changeling to the great tree and switch the changeling with the real Madison to buy her some time while she carries the real Madison back to Cindy's. That leaves the bait. What gets the Vila out of the den in the first place? But I think I know the answer to that too, even though it makes me break into a cold sweat. I take a deep breath in like Cindy taught me, *one, two, three, four*, hold, *one, two, three, four*, and release, *one, two, three, four*.

Anders is sitting on the flower boxes with Ashleigh when I arrive at school. Though I want to, I know I can't just walk

279

by. They're clearly waiting for me. Anders has his sweatshirt sleeves pulled down over his palms and is chewing at the frayed cuff. I can't help feeling the deep pulse of nostalgia when I see him—for the easy smiles, for the chases through cornfields, for the way he looks at me with a singular focus like nothing else matters.

"Hey," Anders says.

"Hey." I try to sound surly, but I can't. I hop onto the flower boxes beside Ashleigh.

"I have to go . . . clean my locker," she announces loudly. Then it's just Anders and me, and a small space between us.

As soon as Ashleigh is out of earshot, Anders turns to me. I can't help but meet his dark eyes. "I really screwed up that apology," he says.

"Both times."

He laughs. "Both times. So I apologize for my apologies."

"And?"

"Hold your horses. I'm getting there."

"Neigh."

He grins and then grows serious again. "This has been hard for me because there are these new things I never thought were possible. And it's made me question, like, everything." He laces his fingers together. "I'm sorry it took me a while to believe you."

"Thank you," I say.

"Can I ask you a serious question, though? If you were in

my shoes, would *you* have believed you?"

I squint at him. The morning sun lights his hair with auburn, and his face is open, his eyes crinkling at the corners. The truth is that I *don't* know if I would have believed me. I could hardly believe what I saw with my own eyes. "You're right," I say quietly. "I probably wouldn't have."

"Wait—what did you just say?" One of his dimples appears. "I was right?"

"Don't push it." We sit for a moment, kicking our legs in and out against the bricks. "I'm sorry I missed your party."

"Me too. It wasn't as fun."

"Oh, I never pegged myself as the life of the party."

"You're the life of my party," he says, giving me an *I know I'm over the top* grin.

"That's maybe the cheesiest thing you've ever said, which is saying a lot."

He laughs. "Come here." He pulls me into a hug. We're in an awkward position, perched on the flower box with our knees angled toward each other, but it somehow doesn't matter because I'm in Anders's arms. "So what's going on with everything?" he asks.

I back out of the hug and explain what's happened with Mr. Kriska and Fanya over the past few days.

"We only have until Halloween," I say.

"Shit," he says.

"Yeah. But I think I may have a plan that will work. If we

can do some sort of bait and switch, maybe Fanya can take the changeling and bring back the real Madison."

"What's the bait?"

I hesitate, my heart kicking off again. "Me."

"No." He shakes his head.

"It's the only way."

He looks at me. "I'll do it."

"No way. I'm not going to let the Vila turn you into a tree," I say.

"Oh yeah, why? You don't like wood?" He lifts and lowers his eyebrows suggestively.

I cringe and crack up at the same time, which I didn't even realize was possible.

"No, but seriously. What will they do to you?" he asks.

"I don't know." I'm not going to make the mistake of telling him what Fanya told me about Nina eating the guts of a creature while it's still alive. I haven't figured out how I'm going to avoid having my entrails torn from my body, but I won't let Anders put himself in danger for me. All I know is I don't have time to worry; I have two days to save my cousin.

And hopefully, Fanya's knowledge will help me figure out what to do.

40

FANYA

I WAKE IN what the fox-furred Mother called a *bed* to the sound of People feet. The bed is softer than any Gray pile I've been in, though not as warm, and I spent a lot of the dark trying to free myself from the long pieces of cloth People Only dress their beds in.

There's a *thud-thud-thud* at the door, and I spring up, hair up on my shoulders. Paws, long and furry, stretch before me. I must have heart-decided Gray in my sleep, which hasn't happened since I was coming into my Forms a long time ago. Dream-switching is the first sign that the ritual of becoming a Vila has worked.

The fox-furred Mother opens the door, holding square objects against her chest. She makes a small cry and jumps back. I forget she hasn't seen my Gray Form.

I change quickly back to People, but that makes her breathe even faster, like fish when you scoop them from the stream in your talons.

"I'm sorry. I didn't mean to scare," I say.

"It's—I haven't seen—it's remarkable."

I show her my teeth, hoping she'll feel better.

"I have to go to work," she says. "So I left you some bacon on the counter downstairs and brought some books." She holds up the square objects. "I wasn't sure if you could read, so they're mostly pictures. And there's TV too." She points at the black box hanging on the wall. "You just press the red button on the remote. The long black thing there."

None of this means anything to me, but I keep my lips pulled back.

"Just make yourself at home."

Home, like my Den? I look around. There is no carcass to roll in or dirt to dig. Everything is too soft and bright.

When she's gone, I try the books first. They smell of trees but also of things I don't know, like so many objects in the People World. The insides are bright and colorful, and everything seems both recognizable and completely odd. In one, flat panels of colors make the shape of a bird, but there are no feathers, no flutter-beating heart, no chirrups. The books hurt too. I keep slicing my fingers on the flaps inside.

I eat the bacon, long salty sweet strips of animal flesh, and try the TV next, poking the red circle on the remote, but the sound is loud—like all the Air Forms screeching at once, and the pictures are too fast, flitting across the box until I feel dizzy.

I push the button so it's over and curl up to sleep.

Later, a *thud-thud-thud* wakes me again. The fox-furred Mother is back, holding the Leftover against her side. It hisses at me, and I growl back, even though I'm in People Form.

"It's Luce," she says, holding up a small shiny rectangle.

"Luce," I repeat, tilting my head. I've seen one of these rectangles before—Luce had one—but I'm sure it is *not* Luce.

"You hold it up to your ear and talk," she says.

I take the rectangle and grip it hard, in case it slips. I hold it up to my face, and the Mother gently turns it over. "Luce?" I say.

"Fanya, I have a plan." Her voice comes from the rectangle. I almost bark in surprise.

Luce tells me I have to take the Leftover, carry it through the forest, run to my Pack's Den, sneak the fox-furred Small out, and carry her back to the Mother's Den.

"How will I keep my Pack from stopping me?" I ask.

"Well, Cindy is going to let me know when you're on your way, and I'm going to go with you to distract them. Like, get their attention somehow so they're not in the Den. I was hoping you might have ideas so that they don't—you know—hunt me or something."

We are taught to stay away from People Only because of their traps and to defend our Den. But Teodora says it wasn't always like this.

"In the Old World," I tell her, "the People Only brought beautiful cloth for us to line our Den with. It was a gift for our protection."

285

"Cloth?"

"With vines and leaves and shiny threads."

"Oh, okay. Got it. I'll have to find something."

"You distract and I will carry, run, sneak, carry, and run," I say.

"Yeah, I know it's a lot. Can you do it?" she asks.

I think of the round-faced, owl-eyed Small clinging to my neck and the fox-furred Mother. The water that ran down her face, and the way she wrapped her long People arms around me. A hug.

I can and will do it for them.

THEY CUT

THEY CUT DOWN our new world trees and filled the land with slow, lumbering cows and fat pigs. They poured seeds into endless rows. Corn. Beans. Corn. Beans. Our pack was diminished after the second trapping. And still we went on. We lived hidden in the shadows of an ever-shrinking forest, without gifts of cloth and promises from heartsick brides. We had to take whatever unprotected baby girl was nearest when the Forefathers' full moon approached. It was what survival of the pack required of us. The only way the gods had left us to carry on.

41

LUCE

Waxing Gibbous (99% visible), Friday, October 30

CINDY TEXTS AT 9:54 that she's about to leave, and I imagine Fanya running down Cindy's driveway, that awful possessed doll in her jaws. Fanya doesn't know how to tell time, so I searched how fast wolves run, and calculated, based on the distance, that it will take her about an hour to reach the log behind our house, and then another thirty minutes for us both to reach the den.

I head to the bathroom, loudly splash water on my face, and run my electric toothbrush, trying to signal to my mother that I'm getting ready for bed. I shut my bedroom door, turn off the lights, and remain fully clothed. I check for the third time that Mr. Kriska's chain and the necklaces from my and Ashleigh's moms are in my pocket—just in case I need them. I keep my eyes open as wide as I can. I can't afford to fall asleep—not that there's much of a risk. I feel jittery and a little nauseated, like the moments right before a test.

I try not to replay what Fanya told me about Nina's hunting—or the Picnic stories of the Vila cruelly singing men into their circles. I picture Anders instead, wondering if he's pretending to be asleep in his own room, the embroidered tablecloths Ashleigh snuck from the drawers of her mom's china cabinet sitting on his dresser. Maybe he's thinking of me too. It's nice to imagine us caught in a parallel moment, even if we're apart.

At 10:15, my mother climbs the stairs. She's nothing if not predictable, especially when she has multiple weddings lined up the next day.

"Luce," she calls softly at my closed door.

I hold my breath. This could be a test. Things are still icy between us, and I miss how simple and easy things used to feel—dinners and dishes and evenings spent on the couch side by side.

"Just wanted to see if you were still awake," she says, and I can tell from her tone that this isn't a test. She wants to talk.

Still, I stay silent. Timing is everything tonight. It's more important that the plan works, and that we get Madison back, than I make up with her. I want my mom to see what I am capable of. I want her to trust me like I am beginning to trust myself.

At 10:50, I put on shoes, open the door, and listen for sounds from my mother's room. Nothing. I close the door behind me, twisting the knob so the door won't make noise. I creep down the stairs and feed a yawning Giblet a *be quiet* cookie just in case.

I extract my jacket from the closet, holding the wire hanger so it won't jingle, and slide out the back door. The security light flips on, but I duck out of it, clinging to the shadows under the overhang of our roof. The night is crisp, cool enough that I can see the puffs of my breath.

I dig through Anders's mom's garden for a pebble and chuck it at his window. It plinks against the glass and falls to the ground. When nothing happens, I try again. This time, the curtains move. I wait with my back glued to his house's siding until I hear the soft click of the sliding door lock. Anders exits, sock-footed and carrying his gym shoes in one hand and the folded tablecloths he picked up from Ashleigh's house in the other. He pushes his feet into the shoes, not bothering to untie the laces, and then glances around the yard.

"Anders," I whisper.

He spins, hand on his chest like I've given him a heart attack. I cover my mouth to muffle a laugh. He makes a face at me, which only makes it harder to keep my composure.

"Shhh," he chides me, his cheeks dimpled with a contained smile.

I join him on the lawn. "You shhh," I whisper back. "Consider it payback for the cornfield."

We cross to the forest together. Once we are inside the trees, I glance back at our houses. Still dark.

"One hurdle down," I say.

"I don't think you're supposed to knock down the hurdles.

Just go over them," Anders says. "But I don't know sports."

I laugh.

He pulls a flashlight out of his pocket, and we navigate our way toward the log, climbing over tree trunks and shuffling leaves. The forest is quieter than usual, the chill seeming to dampen the sounds.

Fanya isn't here yet, so we sit side by side like we did the first night we waited for her. A week has passed, but it feels like forever.

"Milady," he says, passing me the folded cloths. "One for each season apparently."

"I'm sure they'll be pleased," I say, piling them on my lap.

Anders turns off the flashlight; there is no point in wasting the battery when there is nothing to look at but dark trees. I draw my stiff fingers inside the sleeves of my jacket.

"This is the bravest thing I have ever done," I say as a sharp gust of wind nips my cheeks. The branches rustle as though applauding, and then fall silent again.

"Well, you haven't done anything yet, so don't get ahead of yourself," he says. I jab him with my elbow. When I drop my arm, Anders's hand is waiting. There is no question that his hand was open for mine, but it's still unexpected. I withdraw my fingers from the sleeve slowly, practically crawling them across his palm in case he changes his mind. He weaves his fingers between mine and my skin sets fire, despite the cold.

"You're used to being brave," I say. "Standing in front of

hundreds of people and trying to remember your lines."

"That's not bravery," he says.

I want to see his face. "What do you mean?" I ask.

"Well, I like being onstage," he says.

"You like all those eyes on you?"

"Yeah, I do. I don't know if you can be brave doing something you like."

I think about that for a moment. I know I will *like* kissing Anders even though I'm scared of what it will mean for our friendship. That is exactly what makes it a brave thing to do.

I can't waste any more time being afraid. I lean forward, but miss and graze the corner of his mouth with my lips. I almost pull back, but Anders finds my mouth seconds later. His lips are softer than I was expecting, and they seem to call mine forward. My whole body follows, surging against him— hot and cold all at once. Our fingers unlace and he wraps his arm around me. Pressure thrums in my lower abdomen while my skin prickles with goose bumps. I can feel his chest, rising and falling quickly. I realize I've been holding my breath, that I am light-headed with it, but I don't want to stop to gulp in air.

I lift my hand to his cheek and feel the pucker of his dimple. He is smiling. I smile too, and it's like biting into a summer fruit and feeling the sun-warmed juice trickle down your chin.

42

LUCE

ERRRRRRRRR. A SOUND, inhuman like grinding gears, breaks us apart. Anders scrambles for the flashlight and aims it to our right. The beam bounces from tree to tree until it catches the glint of Fanya's gold eyes and gray pelt. The changeling's pajama collar is clenched in her teeth. Not-Madison cries again, *Errrrrrrr.* Fanya sets down the changeling, panting heavily.

"You made it," I say.

She emits a half moan, half whine, like Giblet does when she wants to play.

Anders finds my hand again and squeezes. His pulse is quick beneath my palm. "Are you sure about this?" he asks.

"Yes," I say. I try to sound confident. I may not succeed, but I won't let that fear stop me from trying. Not when my cousin's future is at stake.

"Text me as soon as you can," he says.

I stand and stamp my feet, trying to wake up my numb

toes. I check my phone: 11:03. I glance up at the moon. It looks full to me, perhaps with just the tiniest sliver shaved off the left side. "We better go," I say. I roll the tablecloths under my arm and touch my pocket one more time to make sure the silver chains are there.

Fanya grabs the changeling again and starts down her small tunnel through the brush. I tramp beside them, the flashlight beam bobbing as I climb over and skirt fallen branches. Eventually, I think I can feel the incline of the hill. When my phone shows 11:32, Fanya stops and makes a sound, muffled by the changeling's pj's in her mouth. She sets it down, transitions to human form, and spits a few times.

"Cloth fur," she says. Not-Madison groans and crawls toward a patch of brush. Fanya picks the changeling up again and clamps her hand over its mouth.

"I will wait here or they'll smell me and hear the leftover. Great tree is just through there."

I nod, taking a deep breath to gather my courage.

"Good . . . luck," Fanya says as though trying to remember the word.

"You too."

I start for the tree, glancing back at Fanya once. Her gaze reminds me of when I spotted her at the den before—like she's trying to send a message, not in words so much as in feeling. I will be okay.

I walk up the bare crown of the slope and stop before the

great tree. The wind blows, and the tree's branches bow around me, the skinniest twigs diving, the leaves shaking and falling. It feels like the tree is warning me away.

"Vila," I call, my voice croaking on the word. I try to project like Anders would. "Vila!"

A tawny-colored snake with dark bands comes first, winding right for my feet. Then three wolflike creatures pull themselves out of the hole with their front paws. They stand and shake their fur. They are larger than Fanya. The nearly white wolf with a broad chest and a humped back is the one I've seen before. Another is iron gray but with brown undertones. It is bonier too, its shoulder blades sharp. The last is black and tall, its head almost chest height. It moves lazily like it is dragging its feet through mud. Five falcons follow, taking quick hops out of the den, their wings outstretched as though they are about to take off. Finally, five more snakes slither out, banded and golden brown. I sweep the beam from one animal to the next, so they are spotlit, the dark tree branches a curtain behind them. So many. I wish I could see Fanya for reassurance, but I have to do this part alone.

The first snake slithers in a tight circle, growing taller and fuller with each cycle until she is a human my height. She has opalescent skin that looks pink, blue, and yellow all at once and white hair that hangs in long, twisted curls down her back. She is thin and wiry with elbows and knees like sailors' knots. She moves slowly too—an old woman trapped inside a younger-seeming body.

"Who are you?" she asks. Her words are clearer and crisper than Fanya's and her eyes a paler yellow.

"I'm Lu-Luce." I swallow. "Who are you?"

The Vila seems momentarily thrown to be asked a question. "Teodora," she says. Then, more sharply: "Why are you here?"

The other Vila, I realize, are encircling me, the snakes hissing, the falcons hopping and flapping, the wolves pacing, heads low to the ground.

I hold out the tablecloths like a shield, then lower them slowly to the ground, placing them at their feet. "I brought gifts."

The hissing grows louder, and one of the wolves whimpers in excitement like Giblet when I take out the leash. "How did you know where to find us?" Teodora's eyes narrow. "Was it Fanya?"

"Who is Fanya?" I ask. "No, I know the great-great-grandson of Robya, Anton Kriska."

Teodora shakes her head. "Robya is the one who told the people only where to find us in the second trapping."

"I am so sorry that happened to you," I say. And I really mean it. "I just wanted to show my admiration, like the people in your old country."

Teodora leans down, her eyes glued on me, and grabs one of the cloths, shaking it out of its fold. It's autumn-themed, depicting a cornucopia surrounded by fruits and gourds, all rendered in oranges, greens, dark reds, and browns. She takes

296

another, blue with snowflakes that glitter. A falcon makes an *er-er-er* sound, and I can tell by the way Teodora rubs the cloths between her fingers that she loves them.

Errrrrrrrrr. It's the changeling's grating, mechanical sound again.

"What is that?" Teodora asks sharply. The Vila erupt around me, hissing and growling. Teodora motions, and the white wolf starts for the trees. I have a feeling that this one is the hunter Fanya told me about. A falcon takes off and circles the clearing around the ancient tree.

I have to do something—anything—to distract them from finding Fanya and the changeling. But I've already used the cloth.

"Ooooooo," I moan, remembering the sanctuary. Wolves can't resist the sound of a howl.

The white wolf near the trees gives a little shake as though it is trying to stop itself, but it sinks onto its haunches and scratches at its ears with a back paw.

"Ooooooo," I moan again.

Two of the snakes turn into wolves, one the color of coal and the other a deep granite. The Vila who are already wolves point their noses to the sky. The Vila who are other forms shake away feathers and scales until they are thick-furred and tailed, even Teodora. *Arrooooooo, roooooooo, aooooooooo,* they cry.

They seem to have momentarily forgotten about the sound in the forest, which I hope gives Fanya a chance to get not-

Madison under control and hide somewhere else—as long as she can resist the howl herself.

I stop making sounds, but the Vila carry on around me, ears back, lips pursed. I spin in a slow circle, watching their gray and white and black bodies caught by some unseen force. It's no longer a howl, but a song—haunting and melodious. Their voices now lilting and plaintive. It's beautiful and sad. I know this must be the song that traps men.

The wolves begin to quiet. Teodora shakes her shoulders, a twitch running down her spine to her tail, and begins to transition, her fur absorbing into her opalescent skin. Her ears sink until they are on the sides of her skull and the pointed tips curl in. Her nose shortens, the nostrils blooming outward, and her face rounds until she is human again.

I feel a wet tongue on my calf and spin. It's the white wolf. She wags and begins widening, transitioning into a tall, blocky woman, her hair the color of soot. Her cheeks are a warm pink like my mom's after a glass of wine, and her eyes are the color of buttercups. "I am Nina," she says.

"Hi," I say, offering a hand. Nina takes it in both of hers and brings my knuckles to her nose. I shiver at her breath on my skin.

One of the snakes winds around my ankle. She turns human, a petite girl gripping my leg.

A falcon lands on my shoulder, its talons biting into my skin. They fold in on me then, wolves leaning against my thighs, snakes at my feet, falcons perched on me, humans tracing my fingers like they are something to marvel at.

"So pretty," Nina says, her nose mere inches from mine. I'm starting to feel claustrophobic, and I think there's blood trickling down my collarbone from the falcon's talons.

"Thank you for the gifts, Luce," Teodora says. "What can we do for you?"

I'm not prepared for this question. All I know is that I have to get them farther from the mouth of the den.

"Perhaps there's a lover we can save? A battle to be fought?"

I look at the trees for help, though I know I won't be able to see Fanya's gold eyes from here.

"Hello?" A voice comes from our left, somewhere through the trees. All the Vila freeze. The wolves' ears swivel forward.

"Hello?" the voice calls again.

Anders.

"Hello?" Another voice, this one higher-pitched and full of pep. Ashleigh. How did they find me?

"The stream," one of the human Vila says.

The pack seems to surge in that direction, hands and teeth and talons dragging me with them. The falcon on my shoulder takes off with a tearing sensation that makes me gasp. I stumble-run with Nina, who is still grasping my wrist tightly.

I have no idea what they're going to do. All I can hope is that Fanya has a chance to slip into the den, drop off the changeling, and rescue Madison. *Please, please let this work.*

43

FANYA

I HEART-DECIDE GRAY and grab the Leftover's cloth as the Pack *fwups* and pads and *sssssses* away from the Den. It isn't in Luce's plan, but I see it is my chance. I run faster than ever before. My paws are wings deep inside—like they are also flat People feet and a snake's strong tail.

I run past Great Tree and dive down the tunnel. I pant in the smell of damp fur, dead skin, feathers. My ears flatten. I won't smell it again. There won't be more fur-warm piles or circle sings. No playing after a good hunt or tumble-wrestling at the stream.

I remind myself: The Pack took me too, hid the truth, and scared me away from People Only. The Pack took Small from her Mother and won't give her back.

She is asleep inside her cage. I leap over the sticks, drop the Leftover, and it squawks like a chicken, digging in the dirt with its fingers. The Small wakes, pushing herself to her feet and stumbling toward me. She rings her arms around my neck.

"Doggy," she says. I lick her salty cheek and turn People so I can switch their cloths. That will help keep the Old Ones from noticing the difference right away.

"Mama?" the Small asks as my clumsy fingers fight with the small plastic rounds that snap together.

"Soon," I say. I hope.

I give the Leftover a stick to gnaw to keep it quiet—for now—and change back to Gray. I breathe in my Den one last time. I paw at its wall, leaving a streak of claw marks. Fanya was here. Then I grab Small's new cloth by the scruff. She holds tight to my neck fur with her fists as I tunnel out of the Den and run for the trees as fast as I can.

Who knows where I'll go after I return her to the Mother, but my Pack is not my Pack anymore. My Den is not my Den. So I don't look back.

WHEN THE MOON

WHEN THE MOON swung dark, when the trees dropped their leaves, when the sky cracked into wintery white, when our pack was trapped a second time, we asked: Are we playthings of the gods? Do their laughs ring out to see us fail and falter? To see us penned, our forest reduced and destroyed? Our pack rendered small and weak? Do they want us to seek silver at the hands of men? To choose chains? Have we been made for this very end?

44

LUCE

Full Moon (100% visible), Saturday, October 31, 12:11 a.m.

I AM NEARLY blinded as flashlights swing in my direction. Ashleigh is bundled in a wool peacoat, scarf, and a red hat with a pom-pom. She is holding a beautiful silk shawl with a knotted fringe. The Vila surround her and Anders, leaving only Nina to hold me. I massage my shoulder where the talons pierced my skin. Anders's eyes are the widest I've ever seen them, his brows so high that you can't differentiate them from his swoop of hair. Ashleigh is smiling, her chin lifted, her chest puffed out like she's about to drop her poms and tumble across the end zone. All performance, I'm sure.

Are you okay? Anders mouths. The blood probably makes it look worse than it is.

I nod. *What are you doing here?* I mouth back.

Teodora stalks forward, peering suspiciously at them.

"They're my friends," I say.

"We wanted to meet you and see your powers," Ashleigh says, holding the shawl out.

Teodora takes it but narrows her eyes. "Show us your hands."

Anders puts out his hands, the flashlight flat on his palm. Ashleigh pulls off her mittens. One of the wolves sniffs her palms and she laughs. Anders shoots her a look. "What? It tickled," she whispers.

"Your cloths too," Teodora says.

One of the snakes winds up Anders's leg and slides in and out of his jeans pocket. He looks like he wants to melt into the ground beneath him. I remember the silver in my own pocket and am relieved they didn't search me too.

The snake drops to the ground and returns to the edge of the circle, apparently satisfied. Anders lets out a breath.

I pull my arm gently from Nina's grip and glance behind us. There is nothing but darkness. I wish Fanya and I had thought to create a signal.

"Can you show them how you change forms?" I ask, partially to stall and partially because I want them to see what these creatures are really capable of.

"Oh yes, please," Ashleigh says. "I love magic."

Teodora wraps her arms around herself and seems to cinch inward, her limbs becoming one with her torso, her whole body growing slimmer and smaller. Her skin turns a light tan that almost seems to shimmer, the darker bands undulating as she coils and uncoils. Beside me, Nina drops onto all fours, sprouting thick fur and short fuzzy ears. She stacks herself, broad chest up, like a show dog. Another leaps, changing to a falcon midair and flapping for the treetops. She swoops, high above us, and then falls into a dive that's as precise as a blade. The W formed by the sharp points of her wings and beak and the wide fan of her tail are perfectly silhouetted against the moon.

Ashleigh claps her hands together in what seems like genuine admiration. Anders joins, though he's pale and looks like he might throw up. I can't believe they haven't both fainted.

Seeing my friends' reactions, the other Vila begin to change too, becoming a flurry of feathers and scales and fur and skin. The birds fly and dive. The snakes flick their tails and tongues, shimmy and roll. The humans shout, "Look at me," before they become wolves. They wrestle, snapping at each other's mouths, and woof in excitement.

"Brava," Ashleigh says, giving another clap for the frenzied pack.

Anders tugs my hand and slowly begins to back away. I pull the chain and necklaces out of my pocket, covertly handing one to each of my friends. We back up until we can feel roots under our feet. "On three, we run," Anders says under his breath. "One."

I squeeze his hand.

"Two."

I take a deep breath.

"Three."

I spin, hands out in front of my face, and sprint. I will my feet to find solid ground with each step.

It takes a few moments for the pack to understand what has happened because the only sounds I hear are Anders's breaths on one side of me and Ashleigh making small mewing sounds.

Then: It starts. The birds first—their shapes jets above the treetops. The wolves tear at the forest behind us. There will be no outrunning them. We are too slow and night-blind.

A low branch of a leaning tree strikes me across the abdomen. I fly over it and try to catch myself, but my hands slide on the damp leaves and my chin slams into the ground. The impact reverberates through my teeth, my jaw, my nose. My eyes fill with sparks of white light. I try to inhale, but I can't breathe. I can't move. The crashing in the woods behind us grows closer.

It's over.

Anders grabs one of my elbows and drags me to my feet. I make a dry sucking sound, trying to get air. "Just take a deep slow breath," he says. "You'll be okay. You got the breath knocked out of you." Ashleigh sweeps the woods beside us with her flashlight.

I see a streak of gray. That is enough to jolt me back to life.

"Go!" I gasp.

The Vila run, two on each side of us. I shake the silver

chain to scare them. The wolves fall back the slightest bit, but they don't lose much ground. I've seen videos of wolves hunting before; I know that one will probably move ahead and one will drop behind so we are surrounded. Then they'll pick the weakest or slowest off first.

I keep running, faster than I realized I could, my chest burning from the cold air, my side aching. Each time one of them gets close to my legs, its teeth flashing, I shake the chain at it, again and again, and it falls back a few steps. Anders flicks his in and out, like a tiny whip. Despite the adrenaline, all three of us are starting to slow. I'm not sure what will happen when our bodies force us to stop. Will these tiny chains really keep them from lunging at us?

I have no clue where we are anymore, but I see a light above and ahead that Anders seems to be sprinting toward. A street-light?

We break from the trees onto an empty pad of concrete. It's the cul-de-sac at the end of our unfinished street. The wolves pause and pace at the edge of the tree line, seeming unsure about venturing into the light. I hear a sharp yip. Then another. A small ball of white fur barrels from behind my house and makes a beeline for the wolves.

"Giblet!" I yell. Did I leave the door open behind me when I snuck out?

The wolves' ears stand up and they tilt their heads at Giblet and whine. The falcons circle overhead.

Arf arf arf arf! Giblet hops and lunges but never crosses into the trees. I can't believe this is the same dog who was terrified of the changeling.

Nina paws at the ground, her lips peeled back to reveal long canines. *Errrrrr.*

"Giblet!" It's my mom's voice. She's in her pj's and slippers and is trying to put her arm into the sleeve of a jacket.

She freezes. I can't see her face, but I imagine her mouth open, the V on her forehead a deep valley. Then she charges toward the wolves, as aggressively as Giblet. Our dog unleashes another string of barks, seeming to feel renewed fury now that she's been joined by her owner.

"Go away! Shoo!" my mom yells. "You don't belong here."

Wordlessly, the wolves seem to decide the hunt is over. Maybe it's that they're too exposed, on our turf. Maybe they're afraid of what could happen after, humans hunting and trapping them like in *Picnic's Promise*. They throw one last look over their shoulders before disappearing into the trees. The falcons trail behind them like kites.

"Giblet, you saved us." She trots to me and throws herself at my feet. I crouch to rub her belly.

My mom turns, her mouth an O, seeming to finally register us. "Luce? Why are you bleeding? What on earth happened?"

I glance at Anders, and he nods firmly. It is time for the complete truth.

45

LUCE

WE SIT AROUND the kitchen table, wrapped in fleece blankets. I check my phone, but there's no word from Cindy yet.

Are they back??? I text.

After my mom cleans the talon wound and bandages me, I tell her the entire story: *Picnic's Promise*, meeting Fanya, her kidnapping, our bait and switch, Cindy being in on it, and the chase through the woods. Anders and Ashleigh chime in with details, Ashleigh reminding me that I'd sent her a pin of the location of the den when I first found it. She and Anders couldn't bear the thought of me facing the Vila alone.

Mom listens, chewing on the skin on her knuckle—something I've only seen her do the night we went to the hospital when my grandma fell. Mom occasionally asks follow-up questions, her tone and face neutral. I can't tell if she believes us or not. She just digs her knuckle into her tooth like she is trying to punch her way through.

"All right," she says when we are finished. "I better get Ashleigh home. Anders, hop across the lawn. I assume you can sneak yourself back in?"

Anders's eyebrows shoot up, but he nods. I'm as shocked as he is that she's not going to call his parents.

"But we don't know if it worked yet," I say, checking my phone again. Still no response. "What if Fanya didn't make it back? What if the real Madison isn't home?"

"I know, Luce, but it's late. Ashleigh and Anders have to go," Mom says, standing from the table to grab her keys and purse. "I promise we'll find out what's going on, and you can call them in the morning."

Ashleigh and I wave to Anders and climb into the car. We watch in silence as the dark fields transition to churches, banks, and houses. When we get to her house, Ashleigh says thank you and slips out of the back seat quickly.

It's just Mom and me. Once we are alone, I expect her to start in on me, but she remains quiet, her knuckle back in her mouth.

If she's not going to speak first, I guess I'll have to. "So, how come you were outside with Giblet?" I ask.

"She woke me up," she says. "She kept whining outside my door. I thought she must have to go out."

I don't go so far as to believe Giblet knew she needed to take care of me. Maybe she heard us racing back through the woods and wanted to defend her property like she was some fierce guard dog instead of a roly-poly Frenchie.

Rather than U-turning to head back to our house, my mom turns left. "Where are we going?" I ask.

"To Cindy's," she says. "How else are we going to find out if Fanya and Madison are safe?" She glances at me, a small smile on her lips.

I turn my whole body to look at her. "Wait—so you actually believe me?"

She looks out the windshield again. "Do you remember when you went to Chuck E. Cheese that summer after kindergarten?"

I nod, not sure where she is going with this.

"Well, you tried to lie about being the one who threw up in the ball pit."

I nod. "Yeah, but it was all over my shirt."

"And your face—both literally and figuratively." She snorts and shakes her head at the memory. "Anyway, it was all over your face tonight that you were telling the truth. I don't completely get it . . . but I can tell *you* believe it."

"And you saw them."

"Yeah." She shakes her head. "I thought those wolf things were going to tear Giblet apart."

"It was brave of you," I say.

She glances at me again. "You too."

"So . . . does that mean you admit you were wrong for grounding me?"

311

She laughs. "Don't push it."

We drive past the strip of Picnic's fast-food restaurants, their bright signs reaching high so they can be spotted by drivers on the interstate. "I am sorry, you know," I say. "For lying and sneaking around."

She reaches across the console and squeezes my arm. "I'm sorry too, Luce. You're growing up, and the only way you'll learn to handle the responsibility that comes with more freedom is to have it. I need to practice trusting you and"—she sighs deeply—"letting go a little."

"Thanks. I'd like that."

"There's a lot more to talk about, but I think that can wait."

"Or we could just forget it," I say.

She gives me a side-eye look. "No chance."

All the curtains are closed when we pull up Cindy's driveway. "I don't want to scare her by knocking," Mom says. She pulls her cell phone out of her purse, but before she can dial, the porch lights flick on and Cindy throws open the door, clutching Madison to her chest. My cousin looks half-asleep, rubbing her eyes with small fists. Mom and I climb out of the car and rush to meet them.

I can tell immediately that it's the real Madison. Her hands and face are caked with dirt, but her eyes are like blue sun-catchers.

"It's her. It's her. It's her," Cindy sobs.

"Mama," Madison coos, petting her mom's hair. Hearing her

voice is like the bright shock of diving into cold water on a hot summer day. Madison is home.

We did it.

Mom opens her arms to Cindy, who collapses against her.

"Jan-Jan. Lu-Lu," Madison says. Mom strokes Madison's hair, crying too. I join the hug, holding my mom with one arm and Cindy with the other so that Madison is in the middle of us all.

"I'm sorry I didn't text. They just got here and I was too—" Cindy says between sounds that are either sobs or hiccups.

"It's okay," I say.

"Are you all right?" she asks.

"Couldn't be better."

Madison buries her head in her mom's neck, clearly exhausted.

A figure appears in the doorway behind Cindy and Madison. Fanya, in human form and dressed in Cindy's too-small clothing. I pull out of the hug.

"Mom, I'd like you to meet Fanya."

Mom extracts herself and reaches out her hand to Fanya. Fanya looks at the hand and tilts her head to the side.

"You shake it," I tell her. And she does, but side to side like a dog would shake a toy rather than up and down.

"Fanya, I was so worried," I say.

"You worried about me?" she asks.

"Of course."

She flaps her arms, but then leans against the doorframe, taking it all in, like she's too tired to stand.

"We should let you all get some sleep," I say.

Mom nods. "We will stop by again tomorrow after the weddings."

"All I can say is thank you. Thank you. Thank you. Thank you." Cindy lifts Madison and twirls her in a circle under the porch lights, the gnats spinning above her, like in a waltz.

IN THE SPRING

IN THE SPRING, when the light was green and new, the stream awakened, the ground warmed. And there were new paths, carved through the dead brush by hungry, happy creatures roused from their winter slumber.

We gathered in a circle under the still-cold moon. And we sung on. Still, we sung on.

46

FANYA

I WAKE AT yellow light in Gray Form and follow the sound of Small's *he-he-he-he* down the jagged ridge, out the back door, and onto the caged grass. Small shrieks, wobbles to me, and wraps her arms around my neck.

"Doggy here," Small says. "Hi, doggy." It isn't who or what I am, but it still feels like my name.

The fox-furred Mother shows me her teeth. She is using a tool with fanned twigs on the grass, moving the leaves into one area.

"Come," Small says. The Small runs through the leaves, spreading them out again. They both make happy yapping sounds. It is a game, like the ones I played with Danica and Alina. I try too. Leaves piled. Run run run. Leaves everywhere. Small smacks her hands together.

We do it over and over.

When the Small seems tired, she lies down in the grass,

316

and I lie next to her. She holds my fur in one hand and shoves the other in her mouth. I remember how she held on to me the whole way back to her Mother's Den. Even when limp with sleep, she never let go.

The Mother brings me and Small a cut-up piece of meat she calls a *hot dog*. I wonder if it is made from one like Luce's little rat dog. Either way, it is as salty and delicious as bacon. Way better than squirrel. Even better than deer. I eat it all. Small's lips droop and she wails: "Doggy ate it!"

"It's okay. I'll get more," the fox-furred Mother says.

I sit outside the glass until she brings us more. This time, I let Small eat the pieces first, picking them up with her People fingers and shoving them into her mouth. I want to tell her how slow she is being, but I don't. She tries to feed one of the pieces to the yellow cat, Binky, that wanders into the caged grass, but it sniffs the meat without interest. I eat that piece when no one is looking.

Luce and her Mother come over. I swish my tail to see them, but stay Gray. I feel better that way, and I'm not good at talking anyway. We sit in the Den and I wind myself around their feet.

When the sky goes lavender, the fox-furred Mother puts triangle ears on Small's head and pins a black tail to her bottom.

"Trick-or-treat?" Small asks.

"Yes, it's time," her Mother says.

"Candy. Candy. Candy," Small says, smacking her hands again.

"We're taking her downtown," Luce says. "Want to come

with, Fanya?" She points toward the Night Beast out front.

I flatten my ears, and Luce understands. "Okay, no problem. Say goodbye to doggy," she tells Small.

"No doggy?"

"You'll see her later," the fox-furred Mother says.

Later? Does that mean I can stay? I swish my tail.

They say goodbye and I go back outside, happy to watch the lavender light turn navy and the Forefathers' moon open its eye wide. It is more comfortable on the ground than the over-stuffed bed for People anyway.

I must fall asleep because I wake to a *cheek-cheek-chit-chit-cheek*. Teodora lands on the tree branch. She shakes out her spotted wings and stares hard at me with unblinking eyes. Teodora never chooses Air Form, so that means one thing: They know the real Small is here. I would trade a paw to have heard the Pack when they understood that their own Fanya and People Only had outsmarted them.

Teodora tilts her head. *Scree?* She wants to talk.

I heart-decide People. She changes too, the branch dipping and creaking under her heavier weight. She curls her legs under to hold on.

"Why are you here?" I ask, crossing my arms, trying to warm my bare People skin. Teodora has tiny hills on her skin too.

"You must return her."

"She is not here. But even if she was, I would not give her back," I say.

"The ritual is almost finished." Teodora looks up at the moon. "It's not too late. We just need to bring her to water when the moon is at its highest point."

I shake my head. "She needs to be with her Mother."

"And what will you do? Where will you go?"

I have not come up with an answer yet. All I want is piles of leaves in yellow light and salty hot dogs. "The fox-furred Mother will let me stay."

Teodora bobs her head like she expected me to say that. "Have you thought what you will do when the Small grows up?" she asks. "She will have been raised by People Only. She will want to go do People things like school. She will leave you. Their young always leave."

I paw at my ears. How far do they go? Will Luce go too?

"And even if she doesn't leave you, you know what will happen, don't you?" Teodora's mouth gets sharp at the corners— like when People Only show their teeth, but she doesn't show hers. "She will die and be Gone Forever. They all will."

I paw at my ears again.

"Bring her back to the Pack, Fanya. Help raise her so that she will be with us forever."

"You will let me come back?"

"Yes." She says it fast. Is it a trick? Or does she mean it?

I imagine chasing Small in the woods, wrestling in the dirt, splashing in the stream, curling up in a warm pile in our tiny Den before pink light. In the warm periods, we'll hunt rabbits and squirrel and maybe even deer. I could teach her to be fast and strong like me.

But . . . Small has a Mother who loves her. Like I did. Once.

Small deserves the chance to go to whatever school is and leave if she wants. She deserves to know her People: her Mother, Luce, the Mother of Luce. "What if there was a choice?" I ask. "To be Gray *and* to know her Mother?"

"It is not the Old Way."

"The Old Way does not work," I say. "Maybe it once did. But no more." I see the path through the brush then, what I will do. "When the Forefathers' moon comes again, I will ask Small if she wants to go to the stream to finish the ritual. She can choose to live as People *and* as Vila if she wants. I will teach her." I flap my arms. Maybe Danica and Alina and some of the Young Ones could help me. We could be a Pack of our own, do the ritual ourselves, but only for those who want to be strong and fast and still know their People.

Teodora makes a terrible sound in her throat like hail pelting. It's a fur-up, threatened sound. "You are a fool, Fanya, and you have betrayed the Pack. You may never come back." Her feathers sprout down her forehead and her arms become outstretched wings. *Screeeee*, she says.

I watch her go. It is the last time I will see her, I know. Just like I know that I now get to decide who and what I am. Just like Small. To live like People, to form my own Pack, to roam wild, to do all or none.

47

LUCE

Waning Gibbous (97% visible), Monday, November 2

FOR OUR BREAKFAST, Anders brings two green apples his mother picked from a local orchard. They are crisp and tart, perfect for a fall morning, and we crunch companionably with the windows down. Madison is back, and everything feels right. Friday's rescue mission seems like ages ago. Our kiss does too, as though it is encased in amber from centuries before. A moment locked amid those dark swaying trees.

We chuck our cores into the cornfield for the birds and fall quiet. I wonder if Anders is going to say something about the kiss. Does he regret it? Is he worried about destroying our friendship too? Every time I open my mouth to bring it up, my skin lights on fire, the blotches hot on my chest.

"How are Madison and Cindy?" Anders finally asks.

"They're good. Madison has been sleeping a lot. I think she's still tired from it all."

"And Fanya?"

"Enjoying hot dogs," I say.

He laughs.

"Cindy offered to let her stay, and she said yes. She likes watching over Madison."

"That's awesome." He takes my hand even though it is sticky from the apple. I feel the heat drain from my neck into my fingers. Here we are, clasping hands in the broad light of day, with nothing terrifying looming ahead.

"Hey, so, what is all this?" I ask, holding our hands up so he can see I mean us.

"I don't know. I just . . . I like you. I thought that maybe you and I could—I mean, if that's not what you want or anything—"

"No, it is," I say before he can even finish. "I guess I just wasn't sure what *you* wanted."

"I want it too." His eyes crinkle at the corners so I know it isn't an act.

"So are you, like, worried at all? About our friendship?"

He nods and rubs his chin. "Yeah. I've thought about it a lot. I guess that's what took me so long."

My heart sinks. If we both thought it might ruin our friendship, it's probably best we trust our instincts. Maybe the moments in the forest belong there, preserved in their once-in-a-lifetime magic.

"Here's the thing I know," he says, and I look up at his profile—too anxious to let my heart hope. He puts his blinker on and pulls onto the shoulder. He touches my chin gently so I'll face him. "I know that you will never ever lose me as a friend. Ever. Even if we fight. Even if whatever this is," he says, gesturing between us, "doesn't work out."

"Agreed," I say. "I don't want it to ever ruin our friendship."

He leans over to kiss me, and it tastes of tart apples in cool sunlight.

48

LUCE

MR. KRISKA IS at his desk when I walk through the door, the coffee cup steaming on his stack of papers. When he sees me, he tugs on his ear nervously and levels his glasses on his nose.

"Ms. Green," he says. "You look merry."

"You're back." I'm not sure how to feel.

"When the investigation officially closed, the school didn't have any grounds to keep me at home," he says. "So what—what happened?"

"We saved her," I say. "The real Madison is back."

He smiles—something I've rarely seen. His bottom teeth are crowded close to his lip like they want to escape. "I'm glad." He clears his throat. "And I wanted to say I'm sorry to you and Fanya and Madison."

"Thank you," I say.

"I didn't want to hurt anyone. It's just . . . Picnic has never let me be. I only wanted to be believed—even if for a moment."

I nod, thinking of how I felt when Ashleigh and Anders didn't believe me. I can't imagine how lonely I'd be after a lifetime of Picnic's scrutiny and disbelief.

"It's not an excuse. I know I caused harm."

"I'm sorry we couldn't do something publicly—to show everyone how wrong they were about you." Telling others would risk exposing Fanya, and I promised to keep her safe.

He nods and finger-combs his flyaway hair back. "I've lived this long. What's a little more time?"

"Hopefully a lot more."

He smiles again, but it's pained. "Have you thought about what happens when the next girl goes missing? Or the one after that?"

I have wondered about this. "I guess we'll do what your family did: Tell everyone and pass the story on—no matter what they think. We could even perform the play. That reminds me." I pull the script out of my backpack and hold it out to him. He shakes his head.

"Keep it," he says. "It's your story now."

Mr. Kriska takes our class to the library so we can finish our research fPor the paper. I haven't decided yet how I'll write about this, after all that has happened, but I think I want it to honor the mothers with missing daughters. Those who weren't believed.

I search Rachel's mother, Linda Magruder, née Trappe. I find a photo of her on Picnic Elementary's website where she works as a night custodian. Linda' s face, though, is what stops me. It's heart-shaped, but very long and narrow, with prominent cheekbones. Her eyes are a dark brown, and her hair is too, but I still see the similarity. Fanya. Could Fanya be—? She has to be—Rachel.

I text Cindy. **I need to see Fanya ASAP.**

Everything okay? Want to come over after school?

> **No, now. Can you pick me up? You're family. They'll let you take me out.**

What's even better than a research paper honoring mothers? Bringing a lost child home.

49

FANYA

THE FOX-FURRED MOTHER dresses me in a red triangle-shaped cloth that I pull over my head. She closes it behind me with a *zzzzzpppp*. I like that it leaves my legs free. Less chance to tangle in it.

She and Luce convince me to get in the Night Beast by telling me that we are going to visit someone I might know. We arrive at a large white Den for People. I smell something on the air I know but can't quite remember, like from my foggy memories of Before. I want to turn Gray so I can smell better, but Luce told me to be People. So I follow my weak People nose to a giant orange vegetable with a face carved into it. I press a finger to its skin and remember large hands of a People Only. A man, cutting off the stem. Scooping out the stinky-sweet insides. Handing me toasted seeds.

"It's a jack-o'-lantern," Luce says.

"Jack-o'-lantern," I repeat, now remembering the word and

the way a candle is placed inside so light can shine through.

She takes me to the door and makes the *thud-thud-thud* sound.

A man with white fur on his chin comes to the door. He is bigger than me. The hands hanging by his sides are large, blue veins crawling across them like snakes. The claws are short and wide. The skin is cracked like dried mud. They are hands I think I once saw pulling the stringy guts out of the jack-o'-lantern.

"Rachel?" he asks. "Is that you? You're—Linda! Linda! Come quick!"

"Rachel," I say out loud. Something tiny inside me says, *Yes?* I hear another voice—the same one singing about apple seeds from my memory—*Rach-el, Rach-el, litt-le star, litt-le light.* I can see her then: Long brown fur that piles on her shoulder. Eyes like a starless sky. Delicate fingers that flutter on my cheeks like butterflies. My Mother.

"Fanya, are you okay?" Luce asks.

I'm trying to flap my arms and paw my ears at the same time.

And then the Mother is there, right in front of me. Her fur threaded with silver.

"Rachel," she says, water streaming down her face. "Oh God. It's really you. I'd know you anywhere. We looked for so long."

My cheeks are wet too, but they are also stretched tight so

I can show all my teeth. She folds her arms around me, a hug, and I know this smell too. Like spruce and lilac. My Mother, who loved me, who looked for me.

I feel like I am out of breath, but also like I am soaring above everything, wings outstretched. Free.

ACKNOWLEDGMENTS

I WROTE THE majority of *The Wolves Are Watching* in the darkness and isolation of the initial COVID-19 lockdown, but there's no better reminder of community and light than creating a book.

I treasured drinking tea and chatting about writing over Zoom with my study hall group, Julie Henson, Rebecca McKanna, and Cassandra Sanborn. Their thoughtful feedback shaped the early drafts of *The Wolves Are Watching* and their bright insight helped me problem-solve my way through a difficult rewrite.

The Lund and Acevedo families rooted for me during our weekly video calls. My spouse, Johnny, lightened the load when I was racing deadlines and lovingly tended to our son, Sylvan, whose name—before I even knew it would be his—was written in these pages.

My agent, Sarah Davies, saw potential in this novel when it was just a few chapters and scenes from *Picnic's Promise*. I'm grateful to her for finding supportive homes for my first three novels and for being a tireless advocate.

Liza Kaplan always helps me see my books with a sharper eye and was an incredible partner in revising *The Wolves Are Watching*. Thanks to the teams at Viking and Penguin Random

House for shepherding this novel into the world—especially to Maddy Newquist and Kaitlin Severini for shrewd copyediting and to Jenna Barton and Kristin Boyle for illustrating and designing one of my favorite covers ever.

Finally, thank you to all the readers, librarians, teachers, and booksellers who have read my novels, sent me messages, and tagged me in posts. You help me remember that we are all knitted together.